Fighting For Peace

Henry Van Dyke

Contents

FIGHTING FOR PEACE

BY

Henry Van Dyke

FOREWORD

This brief series of chapters is not a tale

"Of moving accidents by flood and field,
Of hair-breadth 'scapes i' the imminent deadly breach."

Some dangers I have passed through during the last three years, but nothing to speak of.

Nor is it a romance in the style of those thrilling novels of secret diplomacy which I peruse with wonder and delight in hours of relaxation, chiefly because they move about in worlds regarding which I have no experience and little faith.

There is nothing secret or mysterious about the American diplomatic service, so far as I have known it. Of course there are times when, like every other honestly and properly conducted affair, it does not seek publicity in the newspapers. That, I should suppose, must always be a fundamental condition of frank and free conversation between governments as between gentlemen. There is a certain kind of reserve which is essential to candor.

But American diplomacy has no picturesque meetings at midnight in the gloom of lonely forests; no confabulations in black cellars with bands of hireling desperadoes waiting to carry out its decrees; no disguises, no masks, no dark lanterns--nothing half so exciting and melodramatic. On the contrary, it is amazingly plain and straightforward, with plenty of hard work, but always open and aboveboard. That is the rule for the diplomatic service of the United States.

Its chief and constant aims are known to all men. First, to maintain American principles and interests, and to get a fair showing for them in the world. Second, to preserve and advance friendly relations and intercourse with the particular nation to which the diplomat is sent. Third, to promote a just and firm and free peace throughout the world, so that democracy everywhere may live without fear.

It was the last of these three aims that acted as the main motive in my acceptance of President Wilson's invitation to go out as American Minister to the Netherlands and Luxembourg in the summer of 1913. It was pleasant, of course, to return for a while to the land from which my ancestors came so long ago. It seemed also that some useful and interesting work might be done to forward the common interests and ideals of the United States and the Netherlands--that brave, liberty-loving nation from which our country learned and received so much in its beginnings--and in particular that there might be opportunity for co-operation in the Far East, where the Dutch East Indies and the Philippines are next-door neighbors. But the chief thing that drew me to Holland was the desire to promote the great work of peace which had been begun by the International Peace Conferences at The Hague. This indeed was what the President especially charged me to do.

Two conferences had already been held and had accomplished much. But their work was incomplete. It lacked firm attachments and sanctions. It was left to a certain extent "hanging in the air." It needed just those things which the American delegates to the Conference of 1907 had advocated--the establishment of a Permanent Court of Arbitral Justice; an International Prize Court; an agreement for the protection of private property at sea in time of war; the further study and discussion of the question of the reduction of armaments by the nations; and so on. Most of these were the things of which Germany had hitherto prevented the attainment. A third International Peace Conference was necessary to secure and carry on the work of the first two. The President told me to do all that I properly could to forward the assembling of that conference in the Palace of Peace at the earliest possible date.

So I went to Holland as an envoy of the world-peace founded on justice which is America's great desire. For that cause I worked and strove. Of that cause I am still a devoted follower and servant. I am working for it now, but with a difference. It is evident that we cannot maintain that cause, as the world stands to-day, without fighting for it. And after it is won, it will need protection. It must be Peace with Righteousness and Power.

The following chapters narrate some of the experiences--things seen and heard and studied during my years of service abroad--which have forced me to this conclusion. To the articles which were published in Scribner's Magazine for September, October, and November, 1917, I have added two short chapters on the cause of the war and the kind of peace America is fighting for.

The third peace conference is more needed, more desirable, than ever. But we shall never get it until the military forces of Germany are broken, and the predatory Potsdam gang which rules them is brought low.

Chapter I
FAIR-WEATHER AND STORM SIGNS

I

It takes a New England farmer to note and interpret the signs of coming storm on a beautiful and sunny day. Perhaps his power is due in part to natural sharpness, and in part to the innate pessimism of the Yankee mind, which considers the fact that the hay is cut but not yet in the barn a sufficient reason for believing that "it'll prob'ly rain t'morrow."

I must confess that I had not enough of either of these qualities to be observant and fearful of the presages of the oncoming tempest which lurked in the beautiful autumn and winter of 1913-14 in Europe. Looking back at them now, I can see that the signs were ominous. But anybody can be wise after the event, and the role of a reminiscent prophet is too easy to be worth playing.

Certainly all was bright and tranquil when we rolled through the pleasant land of France and the rich cities of Belgium, and came by ship-thronged Rotterdam to The Hague in the first week of October, 1913. Holland was at her autumnal best. Wide pastures wonderfully green were full of drowsy, contented cattle. The level brown fields and gardens were smoothly ploughed and harrowed for next year's harvest, and the vast tulip-beds were ready to receive the little gray bulbs which would overflow April with a flood-tide of flowers. On the broad canals innumerable barges and sloops and motor-boats were leisurely passing, and on the little side-canals and ditches which drained the fields the duckweed spread its pale-emerald carpet undisturbed. In the woods--the tall woods of Holland--the elms and the lindens were putting on frosted gold, and the massy beeches glowed with ruddy bronze in the sunlight. The quaint towns and villages looked at themselves in the waters at their feet and were content. Slowly the long arms of the windmills turned in the suave and shimmering air. Everybody, in city and country, seemed to be busy without haste. And overhead, the luminous cloud mountains--the poor man's Alps--marched placidly with the wind from horizon to horizon.

The Hague--that "largest village in Europe," that city of three hundred thousand inhabitants set in the midst of a park, that seat of government which does not dare to call itself the capital because Amsterdam is jealous--was in especially good form and humor, looking forward to a winter of unhurried gayety and feasting such as the Hollanders love. The new Palace of Peace, given by Mr. Andrew Carnegie for the use of the Permanent Court of Arbitration and its auxiliary bodies, had been opened with much ceremony in September. Situated before the entrance of that long, tree-embowered avenue which is called the Old Scheveningen Road, the edifice has an imposing exterior although a mixture of architects in the process of building has given it something the look of a glorified railway station. But the interior is altogether dignified and splendid, more palatial, in fact, than any of the royal residences. It is lined with costly marbles, rare Eastern woods, wonderful Japanese tapestries, and adorned with gifts from all the nations, except the United States, which had promised to give a marble statue representing "Peace through Justice," to be placed on the central landing of the great Stairway of Honor, the most conspicuous position in the whole building. The promise had been standing for some years, but not the statue. One of my first minor tasks at The Hague was to see to it that active steps were taken at Washington to fulfil this promise, and to fill this empty place which waits for the American sculpture.

Meantime the rich collection of books on international law was being arranged and classified in the library under the learned direction of M. Alberic Rolin. The late roses were blooming abundantly in the broad gardens of the palace. Thousands of visitors were coming every day to see this new wonder of the world, the royal house of "Vrede door Recht."

Queen Wilhelmina was still at her country palace, Het Loo, in Gelderland. It was about the middle of October that I was invited there to lunch and to have my first audience with Her Majesty, and to present my letter of credence as American Minister.

The journey of three or four hours was made in company with the Dutch Minister of Foreign Affairs, Jonkheer Loudon, who represented the Netherlands at Washington for several years and is an intelligent and warm friend of the United States, and the Japanese Minister, Mr. Aimaro Sato, a very agreeable gentleman (and, by the way, an ardent angler), who now represents Japan at Washington. He talked a little, and with great good sense and feeling, of the desirability of a better understanding and closer relations between the United States and Japan. I liked what he said and the way he said it. But most of our conversation on that pleasant journey, it must be confessed, was personal and anecdotic--fish-stories not excluded.

The ceremony of presenting the letter of credence, which I had rather dreaded, was in fact quite simple and easy. I handed to Her Majesty the commendatory epistle of the President (beginning, as usual, "Great and good friend") and made a short speech in English, according to the regulations. The Queen, accepting the letter, made a brief friendly reply in French, which is the language of the court, and passed at once into an informal conversation in English. She speaks both languages fluently and well. Her first inquiry, according to royal custom, was about family matters; the number of the children; the health of the household; the finding of a comfortable house to live in at The Hague, and so on. There is something very homely and human in the good manners of a real court. Then the Queen asked about the Dutch immigrants in America, especially in recent times--were they good citizens? I answered that we counted them among the best, especially strong in agriculture and in furniture-making, where I had seen many of them in the famous shops of Grand Rapids, Michigan. The Queen smiled, and said that the Netherlands, being a small country, did not want to lose too many of her good people.

The impression left upon me by this first interview, and deepened by all that followed, was that Queen Wilhelmina is a woman admirably fit for her task. Her natural shyness of temperament is sometimes misinterpreted as a haughty reserve. But that is not correct. She is, in fact, most sincere and straightforward, devoted to her duty and very intelligent in doing it, one of the ablest and sanest crowned heads in Europe, an altogether good ruler for the very democratic country of the Netherlands.

We settled down in the home which I had rented at The Hague. It was a big, dignified house on the principal street, the Lange Voorhout, which is almost like a park, with four rows of trees down the middle. Our house had once been the palace of the Duchess of Saxe-Weimar, a princess of the Orange-Nassau family. But it was not at all showy, only comfortable and large. This was fortunate for our country when the rush of fugitive American tourists came at the beginning of the war, for every room on the first floor, and the biggest room on the second floor, were crowded with the work that we had to do for them.

But during the first winter everything went smoothly; there was no hurry and no crowding. The Queen came back to her town palace. The rounds of ceremonial visits were ground out. The Hague people and our diplomatic colleagues were most cordial and friendly. There were dinners and dances and court receptions and fancy-dress balls--all of a discreet and moderate joyousness which New York and Newport, perhaps even Chicago and Hot Springs, would have called tame and rustic. The weather, for the first time in several years, was clear, cold, and full of sunshine. The canals were frozen. Everybody, from grandparents to grandchildren, including the Crown Princess Juliana, went on skates, which greatly added to the gayety of the nation.

At the same time there was plenty of work to do. The affairs of the legation had to be straightened out; the sending of despatches and the carrying out of instructions speeded up; the arrangements for a proposed international congress on education in the autumn of 1914, forwarded; the Bryan treaty for a year of investigation before the beginning of hostilities--the so-called "Stop-Look-Listen" treaty--modified and helped through; and the thousand and one minor, unforeseen jobs that fall on a diplomatic chief carefully attended to.

II

Through all this time the barometer stood at "Set Fair." The new Dutch Ministry, which Mr. Cort van der Linden, a wise and eloquent philosophic liberal, had formed on the mandate of the Queen, seemed to have the confidence of the Parliament. Although it had no pledged majority of any party or bloc behind it, the announcement of its simple programme of "carrying out the wishes of the majority of the voters as expressed in the last election," met with approval on every side. The

"Anti-Revolutionary" lion lay down with the "Christian-Historical" lamb; the "Liberal" bear and the "Clerical" cow fed together; and the sucking "Social-Democrat" laid his hand on the "Reactionary" adder's den. It was idyllic. Real progress looked nearly possible.

The international sky was clear except for the one big cloud, which had been there so long that the world had grown used to it. The Great Powers kept up the mad race of armaments, purchasing mutual terror at the price of billions of dollars every year.

Now the pace was quickened, but the race remained the same, with Germany still in the lead. Her new army bill of 1912 provided for a peace strength of 870,000 men, and a war strength of 5,400,000 men. Russia followed with a bill raising the term of military service from three to three and a half years; France with a bill raising the term of service from two to three years (but this was not until in June, 1913). Great Britain, with voluntary service, still had a comparatively small army: in size "contemptible," as Kaiser Wilhelm called it later, but in morale and spirit unsurpassed. Evidently the military force of Germany, which lay like a glittering sword in her ruler's hand, was larger, better organized and equipped, than any other in the world.

But might it not still be used as a make-weight in the scales of negotiation rather than as a weapon of actual offense? Might not the Kaiser still be pleased with his dramatic role of "the war-lord who kept the peace"? Might he not do again as he did successfully in 1909, when Austria violated the provisions of the Congress of Berlin (1878) by annexing Bosnia and Herzegovina, and Germany protected the theft; and with partial success at Algeciras in 1906, and after the Agadir incident in 1911, when Germany gained something she wanted though less than she claimed? Might he not still be content with showing and shaking the sword, without fleshing it in the body of Europe? It seemed wiser, because safer for Germany, that the Kaiser should follow that line. The methodical madness of a forced war looked incredible.

Thus all of us who were interested in the continuance and solidification of the work of the peace conferences at The Hague reasoned ourselves into a peaceful hope. We knew that no other power except Germany was really prepared for war. We knew that the effort to draw Great Britain into an offensive and defensive alliance with Germany had failed, although London was willing to promise help to Berlin if attacked. We remembered Bismarck's warning that a war against Russia and Great Britain at the same time would be fatal, and we trusted that it had not been forgotten in Berlin. We knew that Germany, under her policy of industrial development and pacific penetration, was prospering more than ever, and we thought she might enjoy that enough to continue it. We hoped that a third peace conference would be assembled before a general conflict of arms could be launched, and that some things might be done there which would make wilful and aggressive war vastly more dangerous and difficult, if not impossible. So we were at ease in Zion and worked in the way which seemed most promising for the peace of the world.

But that way was not included in the German plan. It was remote from the Berlin-Baghdad-Bahn. It did not lead toward a dominant imperial state of Mittel-Europa, with tentacles reaching out to ports on every sea and strait. The plan for another Hague conference failed to interest the ruling clique at Berlin and Potsdam because they had made "other arrangements."

Very gradually slight indications of this fact began to appear, though they were not clearly understood at the time. It was like watching a stage-curtain which rises very slowly a little way and then stops. Through the crack one could see feet moving about and hear rumbling noises. Evidently a drama was in preparation. But what it was to be could hardly be guessed. Then, after a long wait, the curtain rose swiftly. The tragedy was revealed. Flames burst forth from the stage and wrapped the whole house in fire. Some of the spectators were the first victims. The conflagration still rages. It will not be put out until the flame-lust is smothered in the hearts of those who kindled and spread the great fire in Europe.

III

I must get back from this expression of my present feelings and views to the plain story of the experiences which gradually made me aware of the actual condition of affairs in Europe and the great obstacle to a durable peace in the world.

The first thing that disquieted me a little was the strange difficulty encountered in making the preliminary arrangements for the third peace conference. The final resolution of the second conference in 1907, unanimously recommended, first, that the next conference, should be held within a period of eight years, and second, that a preparatory committee should be appointed two years beforehand, to consider the subjects which were ripe for discussion, and to draw up a programme which could be examined in advance by the countries interested. That, of course, was necessary. No sensible government will go into a conference blindfold, without knowing what is to be talked about.

But in 1914, when the matter came into my hands, the lapse of time and the negligence of the nations (the United States included) had made it too late to fulfil both of these recommendations. If one was carried out the other must be modified or disregarded. The then Secretary of State, Mr. Bryan, instructed me to endeavor to have the conference called in 1915, that is, within the period of eight years. After careful investigation and earnest effort, I reported that it could not be done at that date. The first thing was to get the preparatory committee, which would require at least two years for its formation and work. Toward this point, then, with the approval of the President, I steered and rowed hard, receiving the warmest sympathy and most effective co-operation from Jonkheer Loudon, the Netherlands Minister of Foreign Affairs. Indeed the entire Dutch Government, with the Queen at the head, were favorable. Holland naturally likes to have the peace conferences at The Hague. They add to the dignity of the country. The honor is well-deserved, for Holland may fairly be called the fountainhead of modern international law, and has produced many of its best expounders, from Grotius and Bynkershoek to Asser. Moreover, as a side consideration, these meetings bring a multitude of visitors to the country, some famous and many profitable, and this is not bad for business. So the movement is generally popular.

My own particular suggestion toward getting the required "preparatory committee" seemed to its author to have the double advantage of practical speed and representative quality. It was to make use, at least for the first steps, of a body already in existence and in which all the nations were represented. But there is no need of describing it, because it did not go through. I was not so much stuck upon it that any other fair and speedy plan would not have received my hearty backing.

But the trouble was that, push as hard as we would, there was no plan that would move beyond a certain point. There it stood still. Washington and The Hague were earnest and enthusiastic. St. Petersburg was warmly interested, but showed a strong preference for its own plan, and a sense of its right to a leading place as the proposer of the first conference. London and Paris seemed favorable to the general idea, and took an expectant attitude toward any proposal of organization that would be on the level and fair for everybody. Berlin was singularly reserved and vague. It said little or nothing. It did not seem to care about the matter.

I talked informally with my German friends at The Hague. They were polite and attentive. They may have had a real interest in the subject, but it was not shown so that you could notice it. They expressed opinions on the value of peace conferences in general which I am not at liberty to repeat. The idea of a third conference at The Hague may have seemed beautiful to them, but it looked as if they felt that it was lacking in actuality. Possibly I did not understand them. That was just the trouble--I could not. It was all puzzling, baffling, mysterious.

It seemed as if all our efforts to forward the calling of the next conference in the interest of permanent peace brought up dead against an invisible barrier, an impassable wall like the secret line drawn in the air by magic, thinner than a cobweb, more impenetrable than steel. What was it? Indifference? General scepticism? Preoccupation with other designs which made the discussion of peace plans premature and futile? I did not know. But certainly there was something in the way, and the undiscovered nature of that something was food for thought.

The next jolt that was given to my comfortable hope that the fair weather in Europe was likely to last for some time was a very slight incident that happened in the Grand Duchy of Luxembourg, to which small sovereign state I was also accredited as American Minister.

The existence and status of Luxembourg in Europe before the war are not universally understood in America, and it may be useful to say a few words about it. The grand duchy is a tiny independent country, about 1,000 square miles of lovely hills and dales and table-lands, clothed with noble woods, watered by clear streams, and inhabited by about 250,000 people of undoubted German-Keltic stock and of equally undoubted French sympathies. The land lies in the form of a northward-pointing triangle between Germany, Belgium, and France. The sovereign is the Grand Duchess Marie Adelheid (of Nassau), a beautiful, sincere, high-spirited girl who succeeded to the crown on her father's death. The political leader for twenty-

five years was the Minister-President Paul Eyschen, an astute statesman and a devoted patriot, who nursed his little country in his arms like a baby and brought it to
a high degree of prosperity and contentment.

Like Belgium, Luxembourg was a neutralized country--the former by the Treaty of 1831; the latter by the Treaty of 1867; both treaties were signed and guaranteed by the Great Powers. But there was a distinct difference between the two
neutralities. That of Belgium was an armed neutrality; her forts and her military
forces were left to her. That of Luxembourg was a disarmed neutrality; her only
fortress was dismantled and razed to the ground, and her army was reduced and
limited to one company of gendarmes and one company of infantry. Thus Belgium
had the right, the duty, and the power to resist if her territory were violated by the
armed forces of a belligerent. But Luxembourg was made powerless to resist; she
could only protest.

Remember this when you consider the fates which fell on the two countries.
Remember how the proud and independent little duchy must have felt beforehand,
standing without a weapon amid the mighty armed powers of Europe.

It was in February or early in March, 1914, that the Grand Duchess sent out an
invitation to the Diplomatic Corps to attend a court function. We all went gladly
because of the pleasantness of the land and the good hospitality of the palace. There
were separate audiences with Her Royal Highness in the morning, a big luncheon
given by the Cabinet and the city authorities at noon, a state dinner in the old
Spanish palace at night, and after that a gala concert. It was then that the incident
occurred. I had heard in the town that thirty military officers from the German garrison at Trier, a few miles away on the border, were coming, invited or self-invited,
to the concert, and the Luxembourgers did not like the idea at all. Well, the Germans came in a body, some of them courteous and affable, the others stiff, wooden,
high-chinned, and staring--distinctly a foreign group. They were tactless enough to
propose staying over the next day. A big crowd of excited Luxembourgers filled the
streets in the morning and gave every sign of extreme dissatisfaction. "What were
these Prussian soldiers doing there? Had they come to spy out the land and the city
in preparation for an invasion? Was there a stray prince or duke among them who
wanted to marry the Grand Duchess? The music was over. These Kriegs-Herren had
better go home at once--at once, did they understand?" Yes, they understood, and

they went by the next train, which took them to Trier in an hour.

It was a very trivial affair. But it seemed to throw some light on the mentality of the German army. It also made me reflect upon the state of mind of this little unarmed country living next door to the big military machine and directly on the open way to France. Yet we all laughed and joked about the incident on the way back to Holland in the train. Only the French, German, Italian, and Belgian Ministers were not with us, for these countries have separate missions in Luxembourg.

At The Hague everything pursued its tranquil course as usual. Golf set in. The tulips bloomed in a sea of splendor. I strove at the footless task of promoting the third peace conference. It was not until the season of Pentecost, 1914, that I went to Luxembourg again, intending to gather material for a report on the flourishing steel industry there, which had developed some new processes, and to get a little trout-fishing on the side. During that pleasant journey two things happened which opened my eyes.

The first was at a luncheon which Prime Minister Eyschen gave me. It was a friendly foursome: our genial host; the German Minister, Von B.; the French Minister, M.; and myself. Mr. Eyschen's wine-cellar was famous, and his old Luxembourg cook was a wonder; she served a repast which made us linger at table for three hours. The conversation rambled everywhere, and there were no chains or padlocks on it. It was in French, English, and German, but mostly in French. One remark has stuck in my memory ever since. Mr. Eyschen said to me: "You have heard of the famous 'Luxembourger Loch'? It is the easiest military road between Germany and France." Then he continued with great good humor to the two gentlemen at the ends of the table: "Perhaps one of your two countries may march an army through it before long, and we certainly cannot stop you." Then he turned to Herr von B., still smiling: "Most likely it will be your country, Excellenz! But please remember, for the last ten years we have made our mining concessions and contracts so that they will hold, whatever happens. And we have spent the greatest part of our national income on our roads. You can't roll them up and carry them off in your pocket!" Of course we all laughed. But it was serious. Two months later the French Minister had to make a quick and quiet flight along one of those very roads.

A couple of days after the luncheon, at the beginning of June, I saw a curious confirmation of Eyschen's hint. Having gone just over the German border for a bit of angling, I was following a very lovely little river full of trout and grayling. With me were two or three Luxembourgers and as many Germans, to whom fishing with the fly--fine and far off--was a new and curious sight. Along the east bank of the stream ran one of the strategic railways of Germany, from Koln to Trier. All day long innumerable trains rolled southward along that line, and every train was packed with soldiers in field-gray--their cheerful, stolid bullet-heads stuck out of all the windows. "Why so many soldiers," I asked, "and where are they all going?" "Ach!" replied my German companions, "it is Pfingstferien (Pentecost vacation), and they are sent a changing of scene and air to get." My Luxembourg friends laughed. "Yes, yes," they said. "That is it. Trier has a splendid climate for soldiers. The situation is kolossal for that!"

When we passed through the hot and dusty little city it was simply swarming with the field-gray ones--thousands upon thousands of them--new barracks everywhere; parks of artillery; mountains of munitions and military stores. It was a veritable base of operation, ready for war.

Now the point is that Trier is just seven miles from Wasserbillig on the Luxembourg frontier, the place where the armed German forces entered the neutral land on August 2, 1914.

The government and the "grande armee" of the Grand Duchess protested. But--well, did you ever see a wren resist an eagle? The motor-van (not the private car of Her Royal Highness, as rumor has said, but just an ordinary panier-a-salade), which was drawn up across the road to the capital, was rolled into the ditch. The mighty host of invaders, having long been ready, marched triumphantly into the dismantled fortress, and along their smooth, unlawful way to France. I had caught, in June, angling along the little river, a passing glimpse of the preparation for that march.

But what about things on the French side of the border in that same week of June, 1914? Well, I can only tell what I saw. Returning to Holland by way of Paris, I saw no soldiers in the trains, only a few scattered members of the local garrisons at the railway stations, not a man in arms within ten kilometres of the frontier. It seemed as if France slept quietly at the southern edge of Luxembourg, believing that the solemn treaty, which had made Germany respect the neutrality of that little land even in the war of 1870, still held good to safeguard her from a treacherous attack in the rear, through a peaceful neighbor's garden. Longwy--the poor, old-fashioned fortress in the northeast corner of France--had hardly enough guns for a big rabbit-shoot, and hardly enough garrison to man the guns. The conquering Crown Prince afterward took it almost as easily as a boy steals an apple from an unprotected orchard. It was the first star in his diadem of glory. But Verdun, though near by, was not the second.

From this little journey I went home to The Hague with the clear conviction that one nation in Europe was ready for war, and wanted war, and intended war on the first convenient opportunity. But when would that be? Not even the most truculent government could well venture a bald declaration of hostilities without some plausible pretext, some ostensible ground of quarrel. Where was it? There was none in sight. Of course the danger of a homicidal crisis in the insanity of armaments was always there. And of course the ambition of Germany for "a place in the sun" was as coldly fierce as ever. The Pan-Germanists were impatient. But they could hardly proclaim war without saying what place and whose place they wanted. Nor was there any particular grievance on which they could stand as a colorable ground of armed conflict. The Kaiser had prepared for war, no doubt. The argument and justification of war as the means of spreading the German Kultur were in the Potsdam mind. But the concrete and definite occasion of war was lacking. How long would that lack hold off the storm? Could the precarious peace be maintained until measures to enforce and protect it by common consent could be taken?

These questions were answered with dreadful suddenness. The curtain which had half-concealed the scene went up with a rush, and the missing occasion of war was revealed in the flash of a pistol.

IV

On June 28, 1914, the Archduke Franz Ferdinand, heir apparent to the Austro-Hungarian crowns, and his wife, the Duchess of Hohenburg, were shot to death in the street at Serajevo, the capital of the annexed provinces of Bosnia and Herzegovina, to which they were paying a visit of ceremony. The news of this murder filled all thoughtful people in Europe with horror and dismay. It was a dark and sinister crime. The Crown Prince and his wife had not been "personae gratae" with the Viennese court, but the brutal manner of their taking off aroused the anger of the people. Vengeance was called for. The two wretched murderers were Austrian subjects, but they were Servian sympathizers, and in some kind of connection with a society called Narodna Obrana, whose avowed object was to work for a "Greater Servia," including the southern Slavic provinces of Austria. The Government of Austria-Hungary, having conducted a secret inquiry, declared that it had proofs that the instructions and the weapons for the crime came from Servia. On the other hand, it has not been denied that the Servian Minister at Vienna had conveyed a warning to the Government there, a week before the ceremonial visit to Serajevo, to the effect that it would be wise to give the visit up, as there were grounds for believing that an assassination had been planned. We knew little or nothing of all this at the time, in The Hague. Anxiously we waited for light under the black cloud. It came like lightning in the Austro-Hungarian note to Servia of July 23, 1914.

It was made public the next day. I remember coming home that evening from a motor-drive through the dead cities of the Zuyder Zee. Taking up the newspaper in the quiet library, I read the note. The paper dropped from my hand, and I said to my son: "That means an immense war. God knows how far it will go and how long it will last."

This Austrian ultimatum was so severe in matter and in manner as to justify the comment of Sir Edward Grey: "Never have I seen one state address to another independent state a document of so formidable a character." It not only dictated a public confession of guilt; it also made a series of ten sweeping demands on Servia, one of which (No. 5) seemed to imply a surrender of independent sovereignty; and it allowed only forty-eight hours for an unqualified, complete acceptance.

Russia promptly declared that she would not object to the punishment of Servians for any proved offense, but that she must defend the territorial integrity and independence of Servia. Italy and France suggested an extension of time for the answer. France and Russia advised Servia to make a general acceptance of the ultimatum. She did so in her reply of the 25th, reserving demand No. 5, which she said she did not understand, and offering to submit that point, or the whole matter, to the tribunal at The Hague. Austria had instructed her minister at Belgrade to reject anything but a categorical submission to the ultimatum. When the Servian reply was handed to him he said that it was not good enough, demanded his passports, and left the capital within half an hour. Germany, vowing that she had no knowledge of the text of the Austrian note before it was presented and had not influenced its contents (which seems incredible, as I shall show later), nevertheless announced that she approved and would support it.

Verily this was "miching mallecho," as Hamlet says. It meant mischief. Austria was inflexible in her purpose to make war on Servia. Russia's warning that in such a case she could not stand aside and see a small kindred nation subjugated, and her appeals for arbitration or four-power mediation, which Great Britain, France, and Italy supported, were disregarded. Behind Austria stood Germany, proud, menacing, armed to the teeth, ready for attack, supporting if not instigating the relentless Austrian purpose. Something vast and very evil was impending over the world.

That was our conviction at The Hague in the fateful week from July 24 to August 1, 1914. We who stood outside the secret councils of the Central Powers were both bewildered and dismayed. Could it be that Europe of the twentieth century was to be thrust back into the ancient barbarism of a general war? It was like a dreadful nightmare. There was the head of the huge dragon, crested, fanged, clad in glittering scales, poised above the world and ready to strike. We were benumbed and terrified. There was nothing that we could do. The monstrous thing advanced, but even while we shuddered we could not make ourselves feel that it was real. It had the vagueness and the horrid pressure of a bad dream.

If it seemed dreamlike to us, so near at hand, how could the people in America, three thousand miles away, feel its reality or grasp its meaning? They could not do it then, and many of them have not done it yet.

But we who were on the other side of the sea were suddenly and rudely awakened to know that the bad dream was all too real. On July 28 Austria declared war on Servia. On the 29th Russia ordered a partial mobilization of troops on the Austrian frontier. On the same night the Austrian troops entered Servia and bombarded Belgrade. On the 31st Austria and Russia ordered a general mobilization.

Then Germany, already coiled, struck.

On August 1 Germany declared war on Russia. On the 2d Germany invaded Luxembourg and France. On the 3d Germany declared war on France. On the 4th Germany invaded Belgium, in violation of her solemn treaty. On the 5th Great

Britain, having given warning to the Kaiser that she meant to keep her promise to protect the neutrality of Belgium, severed diplomatic relations, and on the 6th Parliament, by a vote of extraordinary supply, formally accepted a state of war with Germany, the invader.

So the storm signs, foreshadowed in fair weather, were fulfilled in tempest, more vast and cruel than the world had ever known.

The Barabbas of war was preferred to the Christ of righteous judgment.

The hope of an enduring peace through justice receded and grew dim. We knew that it could not be rekindled until the ruthless military power of Germany, that had denied and rejected it, was defeated and brought to repentance.

Thus those who loved true peace--peace with equal security for small and great nations, peace with law protecting the liberties of the people, peace with power to defend itself against assault--were forced to fight for it or give it up forever.

Chapter II
APOLOGUE

The man who was also a Werwolf sat in his arbor, drinking excellent beer. He was not an ill-looking man. His fondness for an out-of-door life had given him a ruddy color. He was tall and blond. His eyes were gray. But there was a shifty look in them, now dreamy, now fierce. At times they contracted to mere slits. His chin sloped away to nothing. His legs were long and thin, his movements springy and uncertain.

The philosopher who came to pay his respects to the man who was also a Werwolf (whom we shall henceforth call MWAW for short) was named Professor Schmuck. He was a globular man, with protruding china-blue eyes, much magnified by immense spectacles. The fame of his book on "Eschatological Problems among the Hivites and Hittites" was world-wide. But his real specialty was universal knowledge.

Yet on entering the arbor where MWAW was sitting, this world-renowned Learned One made three deep obeisances, as if he were approaching an idol, and stammered in a husky voice: "Highly Exalted!--dare I--?"

"Ah, our good Schmuck!" said MWAW, turning in his chair and recrossing his legs. "Come in. Take place. Take beer. Take breath. Speak out."

The professor, thus graciously reassured, set forth his errand.

"I have come to you, Highly Exalted, to inquire your exalted views on the subject of Lycanthropy. Your Exaltedness knows--"

"Yes, yes," broke in MWAW, "old Teutonic legend. Men become wolves. Strongest and fiercest breed. Eat people up. Frighten everybody. Ravage countryside. Beautiful myth! Teaches power is greatest thing. Might gives right. Force over all!"

"Certainly, Highly Exalted," said Schmuck humbly, "it is a wonder-beautiful myth, full of true idealism. But what if it lost its purely mythical quality and became historical, actual, contemporaneous? Would it not change its aspect? Would not people object to it? Might not the Werwolf get himself disliked?"

"Perhaps," answered MWAW, smiling till his eyes almost disappeared. "But what difference? Ignorant people, weak people, no account. Werwolf is stronger race, therefore superior. Objections silly."

"True, Exaltedness," said Schmuck. "It is the first duty of every ideal to realize itself. Yet in this particular matter the complaints are very bitter. It is said that great numbers of helpless men and women have been devoured, their children torn in pieces, their farms and gardens ravaged, and their houses destroyed by Werwolves quite recently. Shall I deny it?"

"No," growled MWAW. "Don't be a fool. It is too well known. We know it ourselves. We are the wolf-pack. Don't deny it. Justify it. That's your business. Earn your salary."

Schmuck was as nearly embarrassed as it is possible for a professor to be.

"Willingly, Exaltedness," he stammered. "But the trouble is to find the basic arguments. Even among the Hivites and the Hittites, I have not yet discovered any traces--"

"Nonsense," snapped MWAW. "Hivites and Hittites are dead. WE are alive. Justify US. Think!"

"Pardon, Highly Exalted," said Schmuck, "I was trying to think. The first justification that occurs to me is the plea of necessity--biological necessity."

"It sounds good," grunted MWAW. "But vague. Explain."

"A biological necessity is a thing that knows no law. It is the inward urge of every living creature to expand its own life without regard to the lives of others. It is above morality, because whatever is necessary is moral."

"Excellent," exclaimed MWAW. "We have felt that ourselves. Continue."

"Now, doubtless, the Highly Exalted are often hungry."

"Always," interrupted MWAW, "say always!"

"Always being hungry," droned Schmuck, "the Highly Exalted may feel at certain times the craving for a certain kind of food in order to obtain a more perfect expansion. To need is to take. Is it not so?"

"It is," said MWAW, "and we do. Find another argument."

"Self-defense," replied Schmuck.

"Too old," said MWAW. "Worn out. Won't go any more."

"But as I shall put it, Highly Exalted will see a newness in it. The best way to defend oneself is by injuring others. Sheep, for example, when gathered in sufficient numbers are the most dangerous animals in the world. The only way to be safe from them is to attack them and scatter them. Especially the small flocks, for that prevents their growing larger and becoming more dangerous. Particularly should the sheep with horns be attacked. Sheep have no right to have horns. Wolves have none. But even the hornless sheep and the lambs should not be spared, for by rending them you may frighten and discourage the horned ones."

"Capital," cried MWAW, springing up and pacing the arbor in excitement. "Just our own idea. Frightfulness increases force. We like to make people afraid. We feel stronger. Essence of Werwolfery. Give another argument, excellent Schmuck. Think once more."

"The Highly Exalted will forgive me. I cannot, momentarily, bring forth another."

"What!" snarled an angry voice above the trembling professor. "Not think of the best argument of all! Forget your creed! Deny your faith! Wretched Schmuck! Who gave you a place? Who feeds you? Who are WE?"

"The Lord's Anointed!" murmured Schmuck, falling on his knees.

MWAW drew himself up, stiff as steel. His eyes blazed through their slits like coals of fire.

"Right!" he cried. "Right at last. That is the great argument. Use it. WE are the Chosen of God. WE are his weapon, his vicegerent. Whatever WE do is a brave act and a good deed. Woe to the disobedient!"

He held out his hand and lifted the professor to his feet.

"Stand up, Schmuck. You are forgiven. Take more beer. To-night I follow biological necessity. More work to do. But you go and tell people the truth."

So Schmuck went. Whether he told the truth or not is uncertain. At all events, it was in different words. And the Werwolfery continued.

Chapter III
THE WERWOLF AT LARGE

I

In the days immediately before and after the breaking of the war-tempest, the servants of the United States Government in Europe were suddenly overwhelmed by a flood of work and care. The strenuous, incessant toil in the consulates, legations, and embassies acted somewhat as a narcotic. There was so much to do that there was no time to worry.

The sense of an unmeasured calamity was present in the background of our thoughts from the very beginning. But it was not until later that the nature of the disaster grew clear and poignant. As month after month hammered swiftly by, the meaning and portent of the catastrophe emerged more sharply and penetrated our minds more deeply, stinging us awake.

A mighty nation which "rejected the dream of universal peace throughout the world as non-German" (the Crown Prince, Germany in Arms); a nation trained for war as a "biological necessity in which Might proves itself the supreme Right" (Bernhardi, Germany and the Next War); a nation which had been taught that "frightfulness" is a lawful and essential weapon in war (Von Clausewitz); and whose generals said, "Frankly, we are and must be barbarians" (Von Diefurth, Hamburger Nachrichten), while their philosophers declared that "The German is the superior type of the species homo sapiens" (Woltmann); a nation whose Imperial Head commended to his soldiers the example of the Huns, and proclaimed, "It is to the empire of the world that the German genius aspires" (Kaiser Wilhelm, Speech at Aix-la-Chapelle, June 20, 1902)--a nation thus armed, instructed, disciplined, and demoralized had broken loose. Another Attila had come, with a new horde behind him to devastate and change the face of the world. In the tumult and darkness which enfolded Europe, the Werwolf was at large. We could hear his ululations in the forest. The cries of his victims grew louder, piercing our hearts with pity and just wrath.

II

But even when the most dreadful things are happening around you, the regular and necessary work of the world must be carried on. Your own particular "chore" must be done as well as you can do it.

As the trouble drew near and suddenly fell upon the world, the burden of enormously increased and varied duties pressed heavily upon the American representatives abroad. The first thing that we had to do was to make provision for taking care of our own people in Europe who were caught out in the storm and the danger.

That was a practical job with unlimited requirements. No one, except those who had the distracting privilege of being in the American diplomatic and consular service in the summer of 1914, knows how much work and how many kinds of work rushed down upon us in a moment. Banking, postal, and telegraph service, transportation, hotel and boarding-house business, baggage express, the recovery of missing articles and persons, the reunion of curiously separated families, confidential inquiries, medical service (mainly mind-healing), and free consultation on every subject under the sun--all these different occupations, trades, and professions were not set down in our programme when we came to Europe, nor covered by the slim calf-bound volume of Instructions to Diplomatic Officers which was our only guide-book. But we had to learn them at short notice and practise them as best we could. No doubt we often acted in a way that was not strictly protocolaire. Certainly we made mistakes. But it was better to do that than to sit like bumps on a log doing nothing. The immediate affair in hand was to help our own folks who were in distress and difficulty and who wanted to get home as quickly and as safely as possible. So we tried to do it, making use of the best means available, and praying that heaven and our diplomatic colleagues would forgive any errors or gaffes that we might make. We preserved a profound respect for etiquette and regularity. But our predominant anxiety was to get the things done that had to be done.

Take an illustration. Excuse the personal references in it.

From the very beginning it seemed clear to me that one of the greatest difficulties in the first days of war would be to secure a supply of ready money for American travellers in flight. As a rule they carried little hard cash with them. Paper money would be at a discount; checks and drafts difficult, if not impossible, to negotiate in Holland. Moratoriums were falling everywhere as thick as leaves in Vallombrosa.

So I went directly to my friend Foreign Minister Loudon, and asked him a plain question.

"Would your Government be willing to help us in getting American travellers' checks and drafts on letters of credit cashed if I should indorse them as American Minister?"

He answered as promptly as if the suggestion had already been formed in his own mind--as perhaps it had.

"Certainly, and gladly! Those pieces of paper would be the best securities in the world--short-term notes of the American Government. If you will get the authority from Washington to indorse, the Bank of the Netherlands will honor the checks and drafts; and if the Bank hesitates the National Treasury will cash them."

I cabled to the Department of State asking permission to make the indorsements (a thing hitherto expressly forbidden by the instructions to diplomatic officers), and explaining that I would take in each case the best security obtainable, whether in the form of a draft on a letter of credit or a personal note of hand with satisfactory references, and that no money should be drawn except for necessary living expenses and the cost of the journey home. The answer came promptly: "You have the authority to indorse."

So a system of international banking between two Governments was introduced. I believe it was absolutely a new plan. But it worked.

Then another idea occurred to me. The letters of credit were usually drawn on London or Paris. In both cities a moratorium was on. Why not make the drafts directly on New York? Why not call on the signer of the letter of credit for the money instead of calling on the addressee? This would cut out any possibility of difficulty from the moratorium.

This also was a new method. But it seemed reasonable. We tried it. And it

worked. A visiting committee of New York bankers to whom I related this experience later laughed immensely. They also made some remarks about "amateurs" and
"audacity" which I would rather not repeat. But upon the whole they did not seem
shocked beyond recovery.

So it happened, by good fortune, that there was never a day in The Hague
when an American fugitive from the war, homeward bound, could not obtain what
cash he needed for him to live and to get to the United States. But not money to buy
souvenir spoons, or old furniture and pictures. "Very sorry," we explained, "but our
Government is not dealing in antiquities at present. It is simply helping you to get
home as quickly and comfortably as possible. Please tell us how much money you
need for board and passage-money and you shall have it."

Except three or four chronic growlers and a few passionate antiquarian ladies,
everybody took it good-humoredly and cheerfully. I think they understood, though
not always clearly, that our Government was doing more for its citizens caught out
in a tempest than any other government in the world would have done.

When the Tennessee arrived in the latter part of August with $2,500,000 in
gold for the same purpose, it was another illustration of our Government's parental
care and forethought. We received our share of this gold at The Hague. The first
use we made of part of it was to take up the American checks and drafts on which
the Bank of the Netherlands had advanced the money. Then we sent the paper to
America for collection and repayment to the National Treasury. I have not the accounts here and cannot speak by the book, but I think I am not far out in saying
that our loss on these transactions was less than five per cent of the total amount
handled. And we banked for some very poor people, too!

I never had any idea, before the war broke out, how many of our countrymen
and countrywomen there are roaming about Europe every summer, and with what
a cheerful trust in Providence and utter disregard of needful papers and precautions
some of them roam! There were young women travelling alone or in groups of
two or three. There were old men so feeble that one's first thought on seeing them
was: "How did you get away from your nurse?" There were people with superflu-
ous funds, and people with barely enough funds, and people with no funds at all.
There were college boys who had worked their way over and couldn't find a chance
to work it back. There were art-students and music-students whose resources had

given out.

There was a very rich woman, plastered with diamonds, who demanded the free use of my garage for the storage of her automobile. When I explained that, to my profound regret, it was impossible, because three American guest cars were already stored there and the place could hold no more, she flounced out of the room in high dudgeon.

There was a lady of a different type who came to say, very modestly, that she had a balance in a bank at The Hague which she wanted to leave to my order for use in helping people who were poor and deserving. "Please make as sure as you can of the poverty," said she, "but take a chance, now and then, on the deserts. We can't confine our kindness to saints." This gift amounted to two or three thousand dollars, and was the foundation of the Minister's private benevolence fund, which proved so useful in later days and of which a remnant has been left for my successor.

An American wrote to us from a little village in a remote province of the Netherlands saying that his remittances from home had not arrived and that he was penniless. He added by way of personal description: "My social position is that of a Catholic priest with nervous prostration." We helped him and he proved to be all right.

A rising comic-opera star, of engaging appearance and manners (American), who was under a temporary financial obscuration because her company in Holland had broken up, came to ask us to assist her in getting to Germany, where she had friends and hoped to find work. We did it with alacrity. Then she wrote asking us to forward certain legal papers in connection with a divorce which she contemplated. We did it. Then she sent us some of her newspaper articles and a lot of clippings from German journals, requesting us to transmit them in the Legation pouch to America. This we politely declined, with the plea of "non possumus". Whereupon she was furious and denounced us to the German authorities and the German-American press.

An American lady whose husband was dying in Hamburg came in desperate distress with her daughter, to beg us to aid them in getting to him. We found the only way that was open, a little-known route through the northeast corner of Holland, procured the necessary permits, and enabled the wife and daughter to reach his bedside before he died.

A poor woman (with a nice little baby), husband, a naturalized American, was "somewhere in Argentina," wanted to go to his family in one of the northwestern States. She had no money. We paid her expenses in The Hague until we could get into communication with the family, and then sent her home rejoicing.

These are a few examples of the ever-recurring humor and pathos which touched our incessant grind of peace work in war times at The Hague. Thousands and thousands of Americans, real or presumptive, passed through the Legation--all sorts and conditions of men, asking for all kinds of things.

Our house was transformed into an Inquiry Office and a Bureau for First Aid to the Injured. There was often a dense throng outside the front door, filling the street and reaching over into the park. Two Dutch boy scouts, capital fellows in khaki, volunteered their assistance in keeping order, and stood guard at the entrance giving out numbered tickets of admission so that the house would not be choked and all the work stopped.

You see, Holland was the narrow neck of the bottle, and the incredible multitudes of Americans who were scattered about in Germany, Austria, Russia, and parts of Switzerland, came pouring out our way. There was no end to the extra work. Many a night I did not get my clothes off, but took a bath and breakfast in the morning and went ahead with the next day's business. No eight-hour day in that establishment!

It would have been impossible to hold on and keep going but for the devotion and industry of the entire Legation staff, and the splendid aid of the volunteers who came to help us through. Professor George Grafton Wilson, of Harvard, was our Counsellor in International Law. Professor Philip M. Brown, of Princeton, former Minister to Honduras, gave his valuable service. Professor F. J. Moore, of the Massachusetts Institute of Technology, took charge of the registration bureau. Hon. Charles H. Sherrill, former Ambassador to the Argentine, and Charles Edward Russell, the Socialist, and his wife, were among our best workers. Alexander R. Gulick was at the head of the busy correspondence department. Van Santvoord Merle-Smith, Evans Hubbard, and my son ran the banking department. These are only a few names among the many good men and women who helped their country for love.

My library was the Diplomatic Office, to which the despatches and the passports came; the Conference Chamber, where all vexed questions were discussed and decided; the Court of Appeal, where people who thought they had not received fair treatment could present their complaints; and the Consolation Room, where the really distressed, as well as the slightly hysterical, came to tell their troubles. Some of them were tragic and some comic. The most agitated and frightened persons were among the fat commercial men. The women, as a rule, were fine and steady and cheerful, especially the American-born. They met the adventure with good sense and smiling faces; asked with commendable brevity for the best advice or service that we could give them; and usually took the advice and were more grateful for the service than it deserved.

So the days rolled on, full of infinitely varied cares and labors; and every afternoon, about five o'clock, the whole staff with a dozen or a score of our passing friends, went out under the spreading chestnut-tree in the back garden for a half-hour of tea and talk. It was all very peaceful and democratic. We were in neutral, friendly Holland. The big, protecting shield of "Uncle Sam" was over us, and we felt safe.

III

Yet how near, how fearful, was the fierce reality of the unpardonable war! Belgium was invaded by the Germans, an hour or two away from us. At any moment their troops might be tempted to take the short cut through the narrow strip of Dutch territory which runs so far down into Belgium; and then the neutrality of Holland would be gone! The little country would be part of the battle-field. Holland has always been resolved to fight any invader.

All through August and September, 1914, that fear hung over the Dutch people. It recurred later again and again--whenever a movement of German troops came too close to the borders of Holland; whenever a newspaper tale of impending operations transpired from Berlin or London. Once or twice the anxiety rose almost to a popular panic. But I noticed that even then the stock-market at Amsterdam remained calm. Now, the Dutch are a very prudent folk, especially the bankers. Therefore I concluded that somebody had received strong assurances both from

Germany and Great Britain that neither would invade the Netherlands provided the other abstained.

But all the time there was that dreadful example of the "scrap of paper"--the treaty which had been no protection for Belgium--to shake confidence in any pledge of Germany. And all the time the news from just beyond the border grew more and more horrible. Towns and villages were looted and burned. Civilians were massacred; women outraged; children brought to death. Heavy fines and ransoms were imposed for slight or imaginary offenses. (They amounted to more than $40,000,000 in addition to the "war contribution" exacted, which by August, 1917, had reached $288,000,000.) Churches were ruined. Priests were shot. The country was stripped and laid waste. All the scruples and rules by which men had sought to moderate the needless cruelties of war were mocked and flung aside. Ruin marked the track of the German troops, and terror ran before their advance.

On August 19 Aerschot was sacked and 150 of its inhabitants killed. On the 20th Andenne met the same fate and the number of the slain was 250. On the 23d Dinant was wrecked and more than 600 men and women were murdered. On the 25th the university library at Louvain was set on fire and burned. The pillage and devastation of the city and its environs continued for ten days. More than 2,000 houses were destroyed, and more than 100 civilians were butchered. Time would fail me to tell of the industrious little towns and the quaint Old World hamlets that were wrecked, or of the men and women and young children who were tortured, and had trial of mockings and bonds and imprisonment, and were slain by the sword and by fire. Is it not all set down by sworn witnesses in the great gray book of the Kingdom of Belgium, and in the blue book of the committee of which Lord Bryce was the head? Have I not heard with my own ears the agony of those whose parents were shot down before their eyes, whose children were slain or ravished, whose wives or husbands were carried into captivity, whose homes were made desolate, and who themselves barely escaped with their lives?

Find an explanation for these Belgian atrocities if you can. What if a few shots were fired by ignorant and infuriated civilians from the windows of houses? It has not been proved. But even if it were, it would be no reason for the martyrdom of a whole population, for the destruction of distant and unincriminated towns, for the massacre of evidently innocent persons.

Was it the drink found in the cellars of the houses that made the German officers and soldiers mad? Perhaps so. But that makes the case no better. It was stolen drink.

Was it the carrying out of the cold-blooded policy of "frightfulness" as a necessary weapon of war? That is the wickedest excuse of all. It is really an accusation. The probable truth of it is supported by what happened later, when the Germans came to Poland, and when the Turks, their allies and pupils in the art of war, slaughtered 800,000 Armenians or drove them to a slow, painful death. It means just what the title of this article says. The Werwolf was at large.

The first evidence of this spirit in the German conduct of the war that came to my personal knowledge was on August 25. Two or three days before, our American Consul-General in Antwerp, which was still the temporary seat of the Belgian Government, had written to me saying that he was absolutely destitute and begging me to send him some money for the relief of his family and other Americans who were in dire need. The Tennessee was lying off the Hook of Holland at that time, and there were several of our splendid army officers ready and eager for any service. One of the best of them, Captain Williams, offered himself as messenger, and I sent him in to Antwerp, with three thousand dollars in gold in a belt around his waist, on August 24. He had a hard, slow journey, but he went through and delivered the money.

That very night, while he was in the city, a Zeppelin air-ship, the first of its devilish tribe to get into action, sailed over sleeping Antwerp dropping bombs. No military damage was done. But hundreds of private houses were damaged and sixty destroyed. One bomb fell on a hospital full of wounded Belgians and Germans. Scores of innocent civilians, mostly women and children, were killed. "In a single house," writes an eye-witness, "I found four dead: one room was a chamber of horrors, the remains of the mangled bodies being scattered in every direction."

Mark the exact nature of this crime. The dropping of bombs from aircraft is not technically illegal. The agreement of the nations to abandon and prohibit this method of attack for five years unfortunately expired by limitation of time in 1912 and was not renewed. But the old-established rules of war among civilized nations have forbidden and still forbid the bombardment of populous towns without due notice, in order that the non-combatants may have a chance to find refuge and safety. This German monster of the air came unannounced, in the dead of night, and, having wrought its hellish surprise, vanished into the darkness again. This was a crime against international law as well as a sin against humanity.

My captain returned to The Hague the next morning, bringing his report. He had seen the horror with his own eyes. More: with the care of a true officer he had made a map of the course taken by the air-ship in its flight over the city. That map showed beyond a doubt that the aim of the marauder was to destroy the principal hospital, the hotel where the Belgian Ministers lived, and the palace in which the King and Queen with their children were sleeping.

I cabled the facts to Washington at once, and sent the map with a fuller report the next day. I felt deeply (and ventured to express my feeling) that the United States could, and ought to, protest against this clear violation of the law of nations--this glaring manifestation of a spirit which was going to make this war the most cruel and atrocious known to history. The foreboding of a return to barbarism has been fulfilled, alas, only too abominably!

In every step of that downward path Germany has led the way, by the perfection of her scientific methods applied to a devilish purpose.

Take, for example, the use of poisonous gas in warfare. This was an ancient weapon, employed long before the beginning of the Christian era. It had been abandoned by civilized nations, and was prohibited by one of the Hague conventions, for a period of five years. But that period having expired, and the convention being only a "scrap of paper," Germany revived the ancient deviltry in a more scientific form. On April 22, 1915, she sent the yellow clouds of death rolling down upon the trenches of Ypres, where the British defended the last city of outraged Belgium. The suffocating horrors of that hellish method of attack are beyond description. The fame of this achievement of spectacled barbarism belongs to the learned servants of the predatory Potsdam gang. But we cannot blame the Allies if they were forced reluctantly to take up the same weapon in self-defense.

IV

The real character and the inhuman effect of the German invasion were brought home to us, and made painfully clear to our eyes and our hearts, by the amazing tragic spectacle of the flood of refugees pouring out of Belgium.

It began slowly. When the quaint frontier town of Vise, surrounded by its goose-farms, was attacked and set on fire on August 4, there were many families from the neighborhood who fled to Holland. When Liege was captured on the 7th after a brave defense, and its last fort fell on the 15th, there were more fugitives. When Brussels was occupied without resistance on the 20th there were still more. As the invasion spread westward and southward, engulfing city after city in widening waves of blood, the tide of terror and flight rose steadily. It reached its high-water mark when Antwerp, after the Germans had pounded its outer and inner circle of forts for nine days, was bombarded on October 7 and captured on the 18th.

Nothing like that sad, fear-smitten exodus has been seen on earth in modern times. There was something in it at once fateful, trembling, and irresistible, which recalled De Quincey's famous story of The Flight of a Tartar Tribe. No barrier on the Holland border could have kept that flood of Belgian refugees out. They were an enormous flock of sheep and lambs, harried by the Werwolf and fleeing for their lives.

But Holland did not want a barrier. She stood with open doors and arms, offering an asylum to the distressed and persecuted.

I do not believe that any country has ever made a better record of wise, steady, and true humanitarian work than Holland made in this matter. It is not necessary to exaggerate it. Naturally, Belgium and Great Britain bore by far the largest part of the financial burden of caring for the refugees. Regular subsidies were guaranteed for this purpose. But Holland gave freely and generously what was more important: a prompt and sufficient welcome and shelter from the storm; abundant supplies of money for immediate needs, food and clothing, a roof and a fire; personal aid and care, nursing, medical attendance--all of which these bewildered exiles needed desperately and at once.

This is not the place, nor the time, in which to attempt a full report of the humane task which was suddenly thrown upon Holland by the deadly doings of the German Werwolf in Belgium, nor of the way in which that task was accepted and carried out. I shall note only a few things of which I have personal knowledge.

Going along the railway line which leads to Antwerp, I saw every train literally packed with fugitives. They had come, not in organized, orderly companies, but in droves--tens of thousands, hundreds of thousands. They were dazed and confused, escaping from they knew not what, carried they knew not whither. It is well for the poet to say:

"Be not like dumb, driven cattle";

but what can you do in a case like this except run from hell as fast as you can and take the first open road?

The station platforms were crowded with folks in motley garments showing signs of wear and tear. Their possessions were done up in bags and shapeless bundles, rolled in pieces of sacking, old shawls, red-and-white-checkered table-cloths. The men, with drawn and heavy faces, waited patiently. The women collected and watched their restless flocks. The baby tugged at its mother's breast. The little sister carried the next-to-baby in her arms. The boys, as usual, wandered everywhere undismayed and peered curiously into everything.

The crowds were not disorderly or turbulent; there was no shrieking or groaning. There were, of course, some of the baser sort in the vast multitude that fled to Holland--street rowdies and other sons of Belial from the big towns, women of the pavements, and other wretched by-products of our social system. How could it be otherwise in a throng of about a million, scooped up and cast out by an evil chance? But the great bulk of the people were decent and industrious--no more angels than the rest of us can show per thousand.

I remember a very respectable old couple, cleanly though plainly clad, waiting at the station of a small village, looking in vain for a chance to board the train. Everything was full except the compartment reserved for us. We opened the door and asked them to get in. The old gentleman explained that he was a landscape-gardener, living in a small villa with a small garden, in a suburb of Antwerp.

"It was a beautiful garden, monsieur," he said with glistening eyes. "It was arranged with much skill and care. We loved every bush, every flower. But one evening three German shells fell in it and burst. The good wife and I" (here a wan smile) "thought the climate no longer sanitary. We ran away that night on foot. Much misery for old people. Last night we slept in a barn with hundreds of others. But some day we go back to restore that garden. N' est-ce pas vrai, cherie?"

Rosendaal, the Dutch custom-house town on the way to Antwerp, claims 15,000 inhabitants. In two nights at least 40,000 refugees poured into that place. Every house from the richest to the poorest opened its doors in hospitality. The beds and the floors were all filled with sleepers. A big vacant factory building was fitted with improvised bunks and straw bedding. Two thousand five hundred people were lodged there. Open-air kitchens were set up. The burgomaster and aldermen and doctors and all the other "leading citizens" took off their coats and worked. The best women in the place were cooking, serving tables, nursing, making clothes, doing all they could for their involuntary guests.

In the picturesque old city of Bergen-op-Zoom--famous in history--I saw the same thing. There a large tent-camp had been set up for the overflow from the houses. It was like a huge circus of distress. The city hall was turned into an emergency storehouse of food: the vaulted halls and chambers filled with boxes, bags, and barrels. When I went up to the bureau of the burgomaster, his wife and daughters were there, sewing busily for the refugees.

I visited the main hospital and the annexes which had been established in the schoolhouses. Twice, as we climbed the steep stairs, we stood aside for stretchers to be carried past. They bore the bodies of people who had died from exposure and exhaustion.

In one ward there were a score of the most ancient women I have ever seen. They had made the flight on foot. God knows how they ever did it. One of them was so weak that she could not speak, so short of breath that she could not lie down. As she sat propped with pillows, rocking slowly to and fro and coughing, coughing, feebly coughing her life out, she looked a thousand years old. Perhaps she was, if suffering measures years.

Another room was for babies born in the terror and the flight. A few were well-looking enough; but most of them were pitiful scraps and tatters of humanity.

They were tenderly nursed and cared for, but their chance was slender. While I was there one of the little creatures shuddered, breathed a tiny sigh, and slipped out of a world that was too hard for it.

It was part of my unofficial duty to visit as many as possible of the private shelters and hospitals and workrooms and the public camps, because the Belgian Relief Committee and other friends in New York had sent me considerable sums of money to use in helping the refugees. In the careful application of these funds I had the advice of Mr. Th. Stuart, President of the "Netherlands Relief Committee for Belgian and Other Victims of War," and of Baron F. van Tuyll van Serooskerken, a great friend of mine, whom the Queen had appointed as General Commissioner to oversee all the public refugee camps.

Three of these, Nunspeet, Ede, and Uden, were improvised villages, with blocks of long community houses, separate dormitories for the unmarried men and for the single women, a dining-hall, a chapel, one or two schoolhouses, a recreation-hall, a house of detention for refractory persons, one hospital for general cases, and another for infectious diseases. It was all built of wood, simple and primitive, but as comfortable as could be expected under the conditions. The chief danger of the camps was idleness. In providing work to combat this peril the Rockefeller Foundation and the committee of the English "Society of Friends" were of great assistance. Each of these camps had accommodation for about 10,000 people.

The fourth camp was at the ancient city of Gouda, famed for its great old church with stained-glass windows and for its excellent cheese and clay pipes. This camp was the earliest and one of the most interesting that I visited. It was established in a series of exceptionally large and fine greenhouses, which happened to be empty when the emergency came. Somebody--I think it was the clever Burgomaster Yssel de Scheppe and his admirable wife--had the good idea of utilizing them for the refugees. It seemed a curious notion, to raise human plants under glass. But it worked finely. The houses were long and lofty; they had concrete floors and broad concrete platforms where the "cubicles" for the separate families could easily be erected; steam heat, electric light, hot and cold water were already "laid on"; it was quite palatial in its way. A few wooden houses, a laundry, a kitchen, a carpenter-shop for the men, and so on, were quickly run up. There was a bowling-alley and a playground and a schoolhouse. The people could go to church in the town. Soon twenty-five hundred exiles were living in this queer but comfortable camp.

But it was evident that this refugee life, even under the best conditions that could be devised, was abnormal. There was not room in the industrial life of Holland for all these people to stay there permanently. Besides, they did not want to stay, and that counts for something in human affairs. The question arose whether it might not be wise to let them go home. Not to send them home, you understand. That was never even contemplated. But simply to allow them to return to their own country, at least in the regions where the fury of war had already passed by. I suggested to Mr. Stuart that before you allow poor folks to "go home," you ought to know whether they have a "home" to go to. So we took my motor in October and made a little tour of investigation in Belgium.

That was a strange and memorable journey. The long run in the dripping autumn afternoon along the Antwerp Road, where the miserable fugitives were still trudging in thousands; the search for lodgings in the stricken city, where most of the streets were silent and deserted as if the plague had passed there, and the only bustling life was in the central quarter, where "the field-gray ones" abounded; the closed shops, the house-fronts shattered by shells, the great cathedral standing in the moonlight, unharmed as far as we could see, except for one shell which had penetrated the south transept, just where Rubens's "Descent from the Cross" used to hang before it was carried away for safety--I shall never forget those impressions.

The next morning, provided with permits which the German Military Commandant had very courteously given us, we set out on our tour. The journey became still more strange. The beautiful trees of the suburbs were razed to the ground, the little villas stood empty, many of them half-ruined. (Perhaps one of them belonged to our friend the landscape-gardener.) We could see clearly the emplacements for the big German guns, which had been secretly laid long before the war began, concealed in cellars and beneath innocent-looking tennis-courts. The ring-forts surrounding Antwerp were knocked to pieces, their huge concrete gateways, their stone facings, their high earthworks, all battered out of shape.

Town after town through which we passed lay half-destroyed or in complete ruins. Wavre, Waelhem, Termonde, Duffel, Lierre, and many smaller places were in various stages of destruction, burned or shattered by shell fire and explosives. The heaps of bricks and stones encumbered the streets so that it was hard to pick our way through. The smell of decaying bodies tainted the air. The fields had been inundated in the valleys; the water was subsiding; here and there corpses lay in the mud. Old trenches everywhere; thousands of rudely heaped graves, marked by two crossed sticks; miles on miles of rusty barbed-wire defenses, with dead cows or horses entangled in them, slowly rotting, haunted by the carrion crows.

Yet there were some people in the countryside. Now and then we saw a woman or an old man digging in field or garden. We stopped at the front yard of a little farmhouse, where the farmer's wife stood, and asked her some directions about the road. She gave them cheerfully, though the house at her back was little more than a mass of ruins.

"Were you here in the fighting?" we asked.

"But no, messieurs," she answered with a short laugh. "If I had been here, I should not be here. I ran away to Holland and returned yesterday to my house. But how shall I creep in?" She pointed over her shoulder to the pile of bricks. "I am not a cat or a rat."

They are indomitable, those Flemish people. At Lierre we were very hungry and searched vainly for an inn or a grocery. At last in one of the streets we saw a little baker-shop. The upper story was riddled and broken. But the shop was untouched, the window-shade half up, and underneath we could see two loaves of bread. We went in. The bare-armed baker met us.

"Can you sell us a little bread?"

"But certainly, messieurs, that is what I am here for. Not the window loaves, however; I have a fresh loaf, if you please. Also a little cheese, if you will."

"Were you here in the fighting?"

"Assuredly not! It was impossible. But I hurried back after three days. You see, messieurs, some people were returning, and me--I am the Baker of Lierre."

He said it as if it were a title of nobility.

At Malines (Mechelen) the devastation appeared perhaps more shocking because we had known the russet and gray old city so well in peaceful years. Many of the streets were impassable, choked with debris. One side of the great Square was knocked to fragments. The huge belfry, Saint Rombaud's Tower, wherein hangs the famous carillon of more than thirty bells, was battered but still stood firm. The vast cathedral was a melancholy wreck of its former beauty and grandeur. The roof was but a skeleton of bare rafters; the side wall pierced with gaping rents and holes; the pictured windows were all gone; the sunlight streamed in everywhere upon the stone floor, strewn with an indescribable confusion of shattered glass, fallen beams, fragments of carved wood, and broken images of saints.

A little house behind the Church of Saint Peter and Saint Paul, the roof and upper story of which had been pierced by shells, seemed to be occupied. We knocked and went in. The man and his wife were in the sitting-room, trying to put it in order. Much of the furniture was destroyed; the walls were pitted with shrapnel-scars, but the cheap ornaments on the mantel were unbroken. In the ceiling was a big hole, and in the floor a pit in which lay the head and fragments of a German shell. I asked if I might have them. "Certainly," answered the man. "We wish to keep no souvenirs of that wicked thing."

V

I do not propose to describe the magnificent work of the "Commission for Relief in Belgium." It is too well known. Besides, it is not my story; it is the story of Herbert Hoover, who made the idea a reality, and of the crew of fine and fearless young Americans who worked with him. England and France furnished more money to buy food; but the United States, in addition to money and wheat, gave the organization, the personal energy and toil and tact, the assurance of fair play and honest dealing, without which that food could never have gotten into Belgium or been distributed only to the civil population.

Holland was the door through which all the supplies for the C. R. B. had to pass. The first two cargoes that went in I had to put through personally, and nearly had to fight to do it. My job was to keep the back of the United States against that door and hold it open. It was not always easy. I was obliged to make protests, remonstrances, and polite suggestions about what would happen if certain things were not done.

Once the Germans refused to give any more "safe-conduct passes" for relief ships on the return voyage. Of course, that would have made the work impossible. A German aircraft bombed one of these ships. I put the matter mildly but firmly to the German Minister. "This work is in your interest. It relieves you from the burden of feeding a lot of people whom you would otherwise be bound to feed. You want it to go on?" "Yes, certainly, by all means." "Well, then, you will have to stop attacking the C. R. B. ships or else the work will have to stop. The case is very simple. There is only one thing to do." He promised to take the matter up with Berlin at once. In a couple of days the answer came: "Very sorry. Regrettable mistake. Aviator could not see markings on side and stern of ship. Advise large horizontal signs painted on top deck of ships, visible from above. Safe-conducts will be granted."

When this was told to Captain White, a clever Yankee sea-captain who had general charge of the C. R. B. shipping, he laughed considerably and then said: "Why, look-a-here, I'll paint those boats all over, top, sides, and bottom, if that'll only keep the ---- Germans from sinkin' 'em."

From a million and a half to two million men, women, and children in Belgium and northern France were saved from starving to death by the work of the C. R. B. The men who were doing it had a chance to observe the conditions in those invaded countries. They came to the Legation at The Hague and told simply what they knew. We got the real story of Miss Cavell, cruelly done to death by "field-gray" officers. We got full descriptions of the system of deporting the civil population--a system which amounted to enslavement, with a taint of "white slavery" thrown in. When the Belgian workmen were suddenly called from their homes, herded before the German commandant, and sent away, they knew not whither, to work for their oppressor, as they were entrained they sang the "Marseillaise." They knew they would be punished for it, kept without food, put to the hardest labor. But they sang it. They knew that France, and England too, were fighting for them, for their rights, for their liberty. They believed that it would come. They were not conquered yet.

Here I must break off my story for a month. It has not been well told. Words cannot render the impression of black horror that lay upon us, the fierce indignation that stirred us, during all those months while we were doing the tasks of peace in peaceful Holland.

We were bound to be neutral in conduct. That was the condition of our service to the wounded, the prisoners, the refugees, the sufferers, of both sides. We lived up to that condition at The Hague without a single criticism from anybody--except the subsidized German-American press in the United States.

But to be neutral in thought and feeling--ah, that was beyond my power. I knew that the predatory Potsdam gang had chosen and forced the war in order to realize their robber-dream of Pan-Germanism. I knew that they were pushing it with unheard-of atrocity in Belgium and northern France, in Poland and Servia and Armenia. I knew that they had challenged and attacked the whole world of peace-loving nations. I knew that America belonged to that imperilled world. I knew that there could be no secure labor and no quiet sleep in any land so long as the Potsdam Werwolf was at large.

Chapter IV GERMANIA MENDAX

I

The truth about the choosing, beginning, and forcing of this abominable war has never been told by official Germandom.

Now and then an independent German like Maximilian Harden is brave enough to blurt it out: "Of what use are weak excuses? We willed this war, ... willed it because we were sure we could win it." (Zukunft, August, 1914.) But in general the official spokesmen of Germany keep up the claim that their country was attacked and forced to fly to arms to protect herself.

"Gentlemen," said the Imperial Chancellor to the members of the Reichstag on August 4,1914, "we are now acting in self-defense. Necessity knows no law. Our troops have occupied Luxembourg and have possibly already entered on Belgian soil. [A little earlier in the speech he confessed that they had also invaded France.] Gentlemen, that is a breach of international law. The French Government has notified Brussels that it would respect Belgian neutrality as long as the adversary respected it. But we know that France stood ready for an invasion. France could wait. We could not .... The injustice we commit--I speak openly--we will try to make good as soon as our military aims have been attained. He who is menaced as we are, and is fighting for his all, can only consider the one and best way to strike."[1] (The word which Herr von Bethmann-Hollweg actually used was "durchhauen", which means "to hew, or hack, a way through.")

It was against such weak excuses as this, against the vain pretext that the German war-lords were the attacked instead of the attackers, that Herr Harden made

---

1 Out of several translations of this speech I have chosen as the fairest the one printed by the American Association for International Conciliation, November, 1914, No. 84.

the frank protest which I have quoted above.

Meantime the falsehood of the tales of French preparation for invasion and of actual violations of German territory has been exposed by the evidence of Germans themselves. General Freytag-Loringhoven, in his essay on "The First Victories in the West," has shown that the French high command was taken off its guard by the swift stab through Luxembourg and Belgium, and could not get the Fifth Army Corps to the Douai-Charleroi line until August 22. The municipal authorities of Nuremburg have declared that they have no knowledge of the dropping of bombs on that city by French aviators.

The falsehood of the Chancellor's promise that Germany would "make good her injustice" to Belgium after attaining her military aims is foreshadowed to-day. (September 27.) The newspapers of this morning contain a semi-official press statement in regard to a note verbale handed by the Foreign Secretary to the Papal Nuncio at Berlin. Germany, if this statement is correct, now proposes to spoil the future of Belgium by splitting the nation into two administrative districts, Flemish and Walloon, thus injecting the poison-germ of disunion into the body politic. She also demands "the right to develop her economic interests freely in Belgium, especially in Antwerp," and a guarantee that "any such menace as that which threatened Germany [from Belgium!] in 1914 shall be excluded." This is the German idea of making good an injustice by committing a fresh injury. It is in the style of a highwayman who says to his victim: "I will reward you by letting you go. But I must keep the big pearl, and you must permit me to break both your arms."[2]

2   For further confirmation of these ideas see the Memoir of the late General von Bissing, former Governor-General of Belgium, published by the Bergisch-Markische Zeitung, May 18, 1917, and by Das Grossere Deutschland, May 19, 1917.

"History now shows us that, neither prior to, nor at the outset of hostilities, were people able to rely to any great extent on a neutral Belgium, and, should we attach a certain importance to these historic truths, we shall not, however, on the conclusion of peace, suffer ourselves to allow of the revival of Belgium as a neutral state and country. An independent or neutral Belgium, or a Belgium whose status would be fixed by treaties of another kind, will be, as before the war, under the inauspicious influence of England and France, as well as the prey of America, who is seeking to utilize Belgian securities. There is only one way to prevent this, viz.: by the policy of force, and it is force that should achieve the result that the population, at present still hostile, should become used to German rule and submit to it. Moreover, it will be necessary, through a peace assuring us the annexation of Belgium, that we should be able to protect, as we are now compelled to do, the German subjects who have settled in this country, and the protection we shall be enabled to afford them will be of special

Somewhere I have read a Latin line--the name of whose author has slipped my memory--which seems to fit the case perfectly: "Quidquid non audet in historia Germania mendax!"[3]

II
THE AUSTRIAN ULTIMATUM TO SERVIA

In the latter part of 1916 the New York Times published an admirable series of articles, signed "Cosmos," on The Basis of Durable Peace.[4] With almost every statement of this learned and able writer I found myself in thorough accord. But the fourth sentence of the first article I could not accept.

"The question as to who or what power," writes Cosmos, "is chiefly responsible for the last events that immediately preceded the war has become for the moment one of merely historical interest."

On the contrary, it seems to me a question of immediate, vital, decisive interest. It certainly determined the national action of France, Great Britain, and Italy. They did not believe that Germany and Austria were acting in self-defense. If that had been the case, Italy at least would have been bound by treaty to come to the aid of her partners in the Triple Alliance, which was purely a defensive league. But she formally declined to do so, on the ground that "the war undertaken by Austria, and the consequences which might result, had, in the words of the German Ambassador himself, a directly aggressive object." (Off. Dip. Doc., p. 431.) The same ground was taken in the message of the President of the French Republic to the Parliament on

---

service to us in the struggle about to take place in the world's market. It is only by reigning over Belgium that we shall be able to utilize (verwerten), with a view to German interests, Belgian capital in savings and the numerous Belgian joint-stock companies already existing in enemy countries. We ought to have control over the important enterprises that Belgian capital has founded in Turkey, the Balkans, and China. . . ."

3   I have taken the references which follow, as far as possible, from Official Diplomatic Documents, edited by E. von Mach, The Macmillan Co., New York, 1916. The comments and footnotes in this volume are untrustworthy, but the texts are presumably correct, and it is polite to judge the Germans from their own mouths. The book is quoted as Off. Dip. Doc.

4   These articles are now published in book form by the Scribners.

August 4, 1914 (Off. Dip. Doc., p. 444), and in the speech of the British Prime Minister, August 6, the day on which the Parliament passed the first appropriation for expenses arising out of the existence of a state of war (British Blue Book).

The conviction that the ruling militaristic party in Germany, abetted by Austria, bears the moral guilt of thrusting this war upon the world as the method of settling international difficulties which could have been better settled by arbitration or conference, is a very real thing at the present moment. It is shared by the Entente Allies and the United States. It is one of those "imponderables" which, as Bismarck said long ago, must never be left out of account in estimating national forces. It will hold the Allies and the United States together. It will help them to win the war for peace under conditions for Germany which may not be "punitive," but which certainly must be "reformatory".

Understand, I do not imagine or maintain that the primary or efficient causes of this war are to be found in any things that happened in 1914 or 1913. They are inherent in false methods of government, in false systems of so-called national policy, in false dealing with simple human rights and interests, in false attempts to settle natural problems on an artificial basis.

All nations have a share in them. They go back to Austria's annexation of Bosnia and Herzegovina in 1908; to the Congress of Berlin in 1878; to the Franco-Prussian War in 1870; to the Prusso-Austrian War in 1866; to the conquest of Constantinople by the Turks in 1453. Yes, they go back further still, if you like, to the time when Cain killed Abel! That was the first assertion of the doctrine that "might makes right."

But the "occasional cause" of this war, the ground on which it was brought to a head and let loose by Germany, was the Austrian ultimatum to Servia, presented on July 23, 1914, at 6 P. M.

This remarkable state-paper, so harsh in its tone, so imperious in its demands, that it called forth the disapproval even of a few bold German critics, was apparently meant to be impossible of acceptance by Servia, and thus to serve either as the instrument for crushing the little country which stood in the way of the "Berlin-Baghdad-Bahn," or as a torch to kindle the great war in Europe. I do not propose to trace its history and consequences in detail. I propose only to show, by fuller proofs than have hitherto been available, that Germany must share the responsibility for this flagitious and incendiary document.

On July 25, 1914, the German Ambassador at Petrograd handed an official "note verbale" to the Russian Minister for Foreign Affairs which stated that "The German Government had no knowledge of the text of the Austrian note before it was presented, and exercised no influence upon its contents." (Off. Dip. Doc., p. 173.) Similar communications were presented in France and England.

This barefaced denial that the German Government knew what would be in the Austrian ultimatum, or had anything to do with the framing of it, was a palpable falsehood. It was discredited at the time. The antecedent incredibility of the statement has been well set forth by Mr. James N. Beck, in his vigorous book, The Evidence in the Case.[5] New evidence has come in. I intend here to present briefly and arrange in a new order the facts which prove to a moral certainty that the German Government knew beforehand what the content and intent of the Austrian ultimatum would be, and what consequences it would probably entail.

(1) Austria was the most intimate ally of Germany, admittedly dependent upon her big friend for backing in all international affairs. The German Ambassador in Vienna, Herr von Tschirsky, and the Austrian Ambassador in Berlin, Count Szogyeny, were in close consultation with the Governments to which they were accredited during the weeks that followed the crime of Serajevo, June 28-July 23. It is absolutely incredible that Austria should not have consulted her big friend in regard to the momentous step against Servia, altogether impossible that Germany should not have insisted upon knowing what her smaller friend was doing in a matter of such importance to them both. You might as well imagine that the board of managers of a subsidiary railway would block out a new policy without consulting the directors of the main line.

(2) On July 5, 1914, it appears that a secret conference was held at Potsdam at which high officials of the German and Austrian Governments were present. It is not possible to give their names with certainty--not yet, perhaps never--because these gentlemen come and go in the dark. But the fact of the meeting was brought out publicly in the speech of Deputy Haase in the Reichstag, July 19, 1917, and not contradicted. Whatever may have been the ostensible object of this conference, it is impossible to believe that the most important affairs in the world for Austria and

---

5   The Evidence in the Case. Putnams. New York, 1914, pp. 31-46.

Germany at that moment, namely the nature of the ultimatum to Servia and the possible eventuality of a European war, were not discussed, and perhaps decided.

(3) On July 15, 1914, the Italian Ambassador to Turkey, Signor Garroni, had an interview with the German Ambassador to Turkey, Baron Wangenheim, who had just come back from a visit to Berlin. The German diplomat said that he had been present at a conference where it had been decided that the ultimatum to Servia was to be made of such a nature that it could not be accepted, and that this would be the provocation of the war which would probably ensue. Shortly afterward these statements were narrated by Signor Garroni to Mr. Lewis Einstein, attache of the American Embassy at Constantinople, who carefully noted them in his diary.

(4) On July 22, 1914, the British Ambassador in Berlin sent a despatch to his Government which indicated for the first time clearly the attitude which the German Government had decided to take. I therefore quote it in full.

"Last night I met Secretary of State for Foreign Affairs, and the forthcoming Austrian demarche at Belgrade was alluded to by his Excellency in the conversation that ensued. His Excellency was evidently of opinion that this step on Austria's part would have been made ere this. He insisted that the question at issue was one for settlement between Servia and Austria alone, and that there should be no interference from outside in the discussions between those two countries. He had therefore considered it inadvisable that the Austro- Hungarian Government should be approached by the German Government on the matter. He had, however, on several occasions, in conversation with the Servian Minister, emphasized the extreme importance that Austro-Servian relations should be put on a proper footing.

"Finally, his Excellency observed to me that for a long time past the attitude adopted toward Servia by Austria had, in his opinion, been one of great forbearance." (Off. Dip. Doc., p. 56.)

This shows that Germany knew what Austria was doing, approved her plan, and had resolved that there "should be no interference from outside in the discussion"--in other words, Germany would allow no other nation to prevent Austria from doing what she liked to Servia. Could Germany have taken this absolutely "committal" position if she had been ignorant of what Austria intended to do?

(5) On July 23, 1914, the crushing Austrian ultimatum, having been prepared in the dark, was sent to Servia and delivered in Belgrade at 6 P. M. On the same day,

and almost certainly at an earlier hour, the German Chancellor prepared a circular confidential telegram to the Ambassadors at Paris, London, and Petrograd, instructing them to tell the Governments to which they were accredited that "the action as well as the demands of the Austro-Hungarian Government can be viewed only as justifiable. . . . [If the demands were refused] nothing would remain for it, but to enforce the same by appeal to military measures, in regard to which the choice of means must be left to it." (Off. Dip. Doc., p. 60.)

Is it credible that the German Government would have pronounced a judgment so important, so far-reaching in its foreseen consequences, if it had had no previous knowledge of the "action and demands" of Austria?

(6) On July 23, 1914, the French Minister at Munich telegraphed his Government as follows: "The President of the Council said to me to-day that the Austrian ultimatum, the contents of which were known to him, seemed to him couched in terms which Servia could accept, but that, nevertheless, the actual situation appeared to him serious." (Off. Dip. Doc., p. 59.)

How did this gentleman in Munich come to know about the ultimatum, while the gentlemen in Berlin professed ignorance?

(7) On July 25, 1914, the Russian Government was officially informed that: "Germany as the ally of Austria naturally supports the claims made by the Vienna Cabinet against Servia, which she considers justified." (Off. Dip. Doc., p. 173.)

This was a very grave declaration, in view of the public announcement which the Russian Government had made on the same day: "Recent events and the despatch of an ultimatum to Servia by Austria-Hungary are causing the Russian Government the greatest anxiety. The Government are closely following the course of the dispute between the two countries, to which Russia cannot remain indifferent." (Off. Dip. Doc., p. 170.)

Certainly Germany would not have come to the serious decision of giving unqualified support to the claims of Austria as against the expressed interests of Russia, unless she had long known and had full time to consider those claims and what they would involve.

(8) On July 30, 1914, the British Ambassador in Vienna telegraphed to his Government: "I have private information that the German Ambassador knew the text of the Austrian ultimatum to Servia before it was despatched, and telegraphed it

to the German Emperor. I know from the German Ambassador himself that he indorses every line of it." (Off. Dip. Doc., p. 330.)

(9) Count Bernstorff, German Ambassador at Washington, published an article in The Independent, New York, September 7, 1914. In this article he answered, officially, several questions. The first question was: Did Germany approve in advance the Austrian ultimatum to Servia? The answer was: "Yes. Germany's reasons for doing so are the following, &c."

(10) The German Government has itself acknowledged that it was consulted by Austria in regard to the attitude to be taken toward Servia, and the possibility of ensuing war if Russia intervened to protect the life of her little sister state. Germany accepted the responsibility and pledged support. "With all our heart we were able to agree with our ally's estimate of the situation, and assure him that any action considered necessary to end the movement directed against the conservation of the monarchy would meet with our approval." (German Official White Book, p. 4; Off. Dip. Doc., p. 551.)

This is a carte blanche of a kind which no great government could possibly give to another without a definite understanding of what it involved.

Here the summary of the evidence that Austria was not playing "a lone hand" ends--at least until further confidential documents and information about secret meetings are dug up.

Meantime the Imperial German Government maintains its plea of "not guilty." It still denies all previous knowledge of, and all part in, the nefarious Austrian ultimatum to Servia which precipitated the world war.

The denial is both impudent and mendacious.

"Credat Judaeus Apella!"

III
THE RUSSIAN MOBILIZATION

It has been loudly asserted and persistently maintained by the Potsdam gang that the cause of this abominable war was the mobilization of Russia in preparation to maintain the sovereignty of her little sister state Servia if necessary. "Germany," it is said, "earnestly desired, from the purest of motives, to 'localize the conflict'"--which means in plain words to let Austria deal with Servia as she liked, without interference--rather a one-sided proposition, considering the relative size of the two parties in the benevolently urged single combat. "But Russia rashly interfered with this beautiful design by declaring that she could not remain indifferent to the fate of a small nation of kindred blood, and by calling up troops to prevent any wiping out of Servia by Austria, to whom Germany had already given carte blanche and promised full support. This was a wicked threat against the life and liberty of Germany. This was an action which rendered the great war inevitable." So say the German authorities.

The subtitle of the official German White Book reads: "How Russia and Her Ruler Betrayed Germany's Confidence and Thereby Made the European War."[6]

This is the Potsdam contention in regard to the cause of the war. The documents indicate that it is a false contention, based upon suppressions of the truth. This is what I intend to show.

I hold no brief for the late Imperial Russian Government. Doubtless it was shady in its morals and tricky in its ways.

The telegrams recently discovered by an excellent American journalist, Mr. Herman Bernstein, and published in the "New York Herald," show that the late Czar Nicolas and the still Kaiser Wilhelm were plotting together, a very few years ago, to make a secret "combine" which should control the world. When that plan failed, no doubt the vast power and resources of Russia, under an absolute imperial

---

6   I quote from a copy of the original pamphlet, given to me with the compliments of Herr von Muller, German Minister at The Hague. Professor von Mach in his Off. Dip. Doc. does not reproduce this title-page.

Government, were regarded by the equally autocratic Government of Germany with jealousy and distrust, not to say fear. No doubt Russia was an actual and formidable obstacle to the Pan-German purpose of getting Servia out of the path of the "Berlin-Baghdad-Bahn".

Grant all this. Pass over, also, the interminable and inextricable dispute about the precise meaning and application of the terms "mobilization," "partial mobilization," "complete mobilization," "precautionary measures," "Kriegsgefahr," an so on. That is an unfathomable morass wherein many deceptions hide. In that controversy each opponent always charges the other with lying, and a wise neutral doubts both. It seems to be true--mark you, I only say it seems--that the first great European Power to order partial mobilization was Austria, July 26, 1914. (Off. Dip. Doc., p. 197.) On July 28 the order for complete mobilization was signed, war was declared against Servia (pp. 272, 273), and on July 29 Belgrade was bombarded (p. 354).

On July 29 Russia ordered partial mobilization in the districts of Odessa, Kief, Moscow, and Kasan, and declared that she had no aggressive intention against Germany. (Off. Dip. Doc., p. 294.) The Russian preparations obviously had relation only to Austria's war on Servia which was already under way.

On July 30 Germany had effected her "covering dispositions" of troops along the French border, from Luxembourg to the Vosges, part of which by chance I saw in June (see p. 36 ff.), and on the same day the Berlin semi-official press announced that a complete mobilization had been ordered. (Off. Dip. Doc., pp. 324, 342.) This announcement was contradicted and withdrawn later on the same day by government orders.

On July 31, at 1 a.m., the Austrian order of complete mobilization, which was signed on the 28th, was issued. (Off. Dip. Doc., p. 356.) Later in the same day the Russian Government ordered complete mobilization and the German Government proclaimed a state of Kriegsgefahr, "wardanger." (Off. Dip. Doc., pp. 356-357.) At seven o'clock in the evening of the same day Germany sent an ultimatum to France, and at midnight an ultimatum to Russia.

On August 1 she declared war on Russia, and on August 3 she declared war on France, having previously invaded French territory and sent her army through neutral Luxembourg.

Now in all this the German Government tries to make it appear that it was simply acting on the defensive, taking necessary steps to guard against the peril threatened by the military measures of Russia.

The falsity of this pretense is easily shown from two facts: First, the Russian Government was all the time pleading for a peaceful settlement of the Austro-Servian dispute, by arbitration, or by a four-power conference. Second, definite offers were made to halt the Russian military measures at once on conditions most favorable to Austria, if Austria and Germany would agree to an examination by the Great Powers of Austria's just claims on Servia.

On the first point, I do not propose to retell the long story of the efforts supported by France, England, Italy, and Russia herself, to get Germany to consent to some plan, any plan, which might avert war by an appeal to reason and justice. To these efforts Germany answered in effect that she could not "coerce" her ally Austria.

But one document in this line seems to me particularly interesting--even pathetic. It is a telegram sent by the late Czar Nicolas to his Imperial Cousin, Kaiser Wilhelm. It is dated July 29, 1914, and reads as follows:

"Thanks for your telegram which is conciliatory and friendly, whereas the official message presented to-day by your Ambassador to my Minister was conveyed in a very different tone. I beg you to explain this divergency. It would be right to give over the Austro-Servian problem to The Hague Tribunal. I trust in your wisdom and friendship."

"NICOLAS."

This telegram is not contained in the "German White Book." But Professor von Mach gives it in his "Official Diplomatic Documents" (p. 596).

I have been unable to find in any book, pamphlet, or collection of papers a trace of the Kaiser's answer. Probably he did not send one.

On the second point I propose to quote only the three definite proposals which were before the German Government on July 31, 1914.

Sir Edward Grey, the British Secretary for Foreign Affairs, had been trying with the cordial help of the Russian Foreign Minister, Sazonof, and the President of the Council of France, M. Viviani, to formulate a plan of averting general hostilities which would meet the approval of Germany.

(1) On July 29 Sir E. Grey had an official conversation with the German Ambassador in London and laid before him a proposal in regard to the halting of military measures, described in the following words:

"It was of course too late for all military operations against Servia to be suspended. In a short time, I supposed, the Austrian forces would be in Belgrade, and in occupation of some Servian territory. But even then it might be possible to bring some mediation into existence if Austria, while saying that she must hold the occupied territory until she had complete satisfaction from Servia, stated that she would not advance further, pending an effort of the Powers to mediate between her and Russia." (Off. Dip. Doc., p. 307.) This proposal was telegraphed to Berlin on the same day, and from there to Vienna. So far as I know no answer to it has ever been received, though King George V warmly supported the proposal in a personal telegram (July 30) to Prince Henry of Prussia, and begged him to urge it upon the Kaiser.

(2) On July 30 Sazonof in the name of the Czar presented to the German Ambassador at Petrograd, and telegraphed for delivery to the Foreign Offices at Berlin and Vienna, the following proposal:

"If Austria, recognizing that the Austro-Servian question has assumed the character of a question of European interest, declares herself ready to eliminate from her ultimatum points which violate the sovereign rights of Servia, Russia undertakes to stop her military preparations." (Off. Dip. Doc., p. 341.)

The German Foreign Minister von Jagow, without waiting to consult Vienna, replied "that he considered it impossible for Austria to accept the proposal." (Ibid., p. 342.) Austria said nothing at all!

(3) On July 31 practically the same proposal, modified on the suggestion of Sir E. Grey and M. Viviani, was renewed by Russia. As presented to Berlin and Vienna it read as follows:

"If Austria consents to stay the march of her troops on Servian territory; and if, recognizing that the Austro-Servian conflict has assumed the character of a question of European interest, she admits that the Great Powers may examine the satisfaction which Servia can accord to the Austro-Hungarian Government without injury to her rights as a sovereign State or her independence, Russia undertakes to maintain her expectant attitude." (Off. Dip. Doc., p. 370.)

No answer from Austria, who had ordered a general mobilization at one o'clock in the morning of that day!

No answer from Germany, except the prompt proclamation of Kriegsgefahr, and the declaration of war on Russia on August 1!

Thus three successive opportunities of putting a stop to further military preparations of Russia on the simple condition that Austria would go no further, but be content with what she already had occupied as a guarantee for reparation from Servia--three golden occasions of preserving the peace of Europe--were brushed aside by Germany practically without consideration.

Yet the marvellous people at Potsdam go on saying that it was the Russian military preparation that brought this war down on the world!--that Germany always wanted peace, and worked for it!

Why then did she not accept the proffered chance of staying the progress of Russian preparations when it lay within her power to do so by lifting a finger?

Because she did not wish the chance. Because she wished Austria to go on with the subjugation of Servia. Because she wished Russia to be forced to go on with her measures to intervene for the rescue of Servia from extinction. Because she wished herself to go on with her design of putting her own incomparable military machine at work to force her will on Europe. Because she wished to have a false excuse to cover her own guilt in making the war by saying: "Russia did it."

The Potsdam gang forgot one thing. Most liars forget something.

They forgot that by refusing the opportunity for peaceful settlement which would have removed their excuse for making war, they would furnish the proof that their excuse was false.

Chapter V
A DIALOGUE ON PEACE BETWEEN A HOUSEHOLDER AND A BURGLAR

The house was badly wrecked by the struggle which had raged through it. The walls were marred, the windows and mirrors shattered, the pictures ruined, the furniture smashed into kindling-wood.

Worst of all, the faithful servants and some of the children were lying in dark corners, dead or grievously wounded.

The Burglar who had wrought the damage sat in the middle of the dining-room floor, with his swag around him. It was neatly arranged in bags, for in spite of his madness he was a most methodical man. One bag was labelled silverware; another, jewels; another, cash; and another, souvenirs. There was blood on his hands and a fatuous smile on his face.

"Surely I am a mighty man," he said to himself, "and I have proved it! But I am very tired, as well as kind-hearted, and I feel that it is now time to begin a Conversation on Peace."

The Householder, who was also something of a Pacifist on appropriate occasions, but never a blind one, stood near. Through the brief lull in the rampage he overheard the mutterings of the Burglar.

"'Were you speaking to me?" he asked. "As a matter of fact," answered the Burglar, "I was talking to myself. But it is the same thing. Are we not brothers? Do we not both love Peace? Come sit beside me, and let us talk about it."

"What do you mean by Peace," said the Householder, looking grimly around him; "do you mean all this?"

"No, no," said the Burglar; "that is--er--not exactly! 'All this' is most regrettable. I weep over it. If I could have had my way unopposed it would never have happened. But until you sit down close beside me I really cannot tell you in particular what I mean by that blessed word Peace. In general, I mean something like the status quo ante bel-"

"In this case," interrupted the Householder, "you should say the status quo ante furtum--not bellum [the state of things before the burglary, not before the war], You are a mighty robber--not a common thief, but a most uncommon one. Do you mean to restore the plunder you have grabbed?"

"Yes, certainly," replied the Burglar, in a magnanimous tone; "that is to say, I mean you shall have a part of it, freely and willingly. I could keep it all, you know, but I am too noble to do that. You shall take the silverware and the souvenirs, I will take the jewels and the cash. Isn't that a fair division? Peace must always stand on a basis of equality between the two parties. Shake hands on it."

The Householder put his hand behind his back.

"You insult me," said he. "If I were your equal I should die of shame. Waive the comparison. What about the damage you have done here? Who shall repair it?"

"All the world," cried the Burglar eagerly; "everybody will help--especially your big neighbor across the lake. He is a fool with plenty of money. You cannot expect me to contribute. I am poor, but as honest as my profession will permit. This damage in your house is not wilful injury. It is merely one of the necessary accompaniments of my practice of burglary. You ought not to feel sore about it. Why do you call attention to it, instead of talking politely and earnestly about the blessings of Peace?"

"I am talking to you as politely as I can," said the Householder, moistening his dry lips, "but while I am doing it, I feel as if I were smeared with mud. Tell me, what have you to say about my children and my servants whom you have tortured and murdered?"

"Ah, that," answered the Burglar, shrugging his shoulders and spreading out his hands, palms upward, so that he looked like a gigantic toad, "--that indeed is so very, very sad! My heart mourns over it. But how could it be avoided? Those foolish people would not lie down, would not be still. Their conduct was directly contrary to my system; see section 417, chapter 93, in my 'Great Field-Book of Burglary,' under the title 'Schrecklichkeit.' Perhaps in the excitement of the moment I went a little beyond those scientific regulations. The babies need not have been killed--only terrified. But that was a mere error of judgment which you will readily forgive and forget for the sake of the holy cause of Peace. Will you not?"

The Householder turned quickly and spat into the fireplace.

"Blasphemer," he cried, "my gorge rises at you! Can there be any forgiveness until you repent? Can there be any Peace in the world if you go loose in it, ready to break and enter and kill when it pleases you? Will you lay down your weapons and come before the Judge?"

The Burglar rose slowly to his feet, twisting up his mustache with bloody brass-knuckled hands.

"You are a colossal ass," he growled. "You forget how strong I am, how much I can still hurt you. I have offered you a chance to get Peace. Don't you want it?"

"Not as a present from you," said the Householder slowly. "It would poison me. I would rather die a decent man's death."

He went a step nearer to the Burglar, who quickly backed away.

"Come," the Householder continued, "let us bandy compliments no longer. You are where you have no right to be. You can talk when I get you before the Judge. I want Peace no more than I want Justice. While there is a God in heaven and honest freemen still live on earth I will fight for both."

He took a fresh grip on his club, and the Burglar backed again, ready to spring.

Through the dead silence of the room there came a loud knocking at the door. Could it be the big neighbor from across the lake?

Chapter VI
STAND FAST, YE FREE!

I

From the outset of this war two things have been clear to me.

First, if the war continued it was absolutely inevitable that the United States would be either drawn into it by the impulse of democratic sympathies or forced into it by the instinct of self-preservation.

Second, the most adequate person in the world to decide when and how the United States should accept the great responsibility of fighting beside France and Great Britain for peace and for the American ideal of freedom was President Wilson.

His sagacity, his patience, his knowledge of the varied elements that are blended in our nationality, his sincere devotion to pacific conceptions of progress, his unwavering loyalty to the cause of liberty secured by law, national and international, made him the one man of all others to whom this great decision could most safely be confided.

The people of the United States believed this in the election of 1916. They trusted him sincerely then because "he kept us out of the war" until the inevitable hour. No less sincerely do they trust him now when he declares that the hour has come when we must "dedicate our lives and our fortunes, everything that we are and everything that we have" (President's Message to Congress, April 2, 1917), to defend ourselves and the world from the Imperial German Government, which is waging "a warfare against mankind."

In the quiet, but never idle, American Legation at The Hague there was an excellent opportunity to observe and study the incredible blunders by which Germany led us, and the unspeakable insults and injuries by which she compelled us, to enter the war.

Our adherence to the Monroe Doctrine was, at first, an obstacle to that entrance. Believing that European governments ought not to interfere in domestic affairs on the American continents, we admitted the converse of that proposition, and held that America should not meddle with European controversies or conflicts. But we soon came to a realizing sense of the ominous fact that Germany was the one nation of Europe which openly despised and flouted the Monroe Doctrine as an outworn superstition. Her learned professors (followed by a few servile American imitators) had poured ridicule and scorn upon it in unreadable books. Her actions in the West Indies and South America showed her contempt for it as a "bit of American bluff." Gradually it dawned upon us that if France were crushed and England crippled our dear old Monroe Doctrine would stand a poor chance against a victorious and supercilious Imperial German Government. As I wrote to Washington in August, 1914, their idea was to "lunch in Paris, dine in London, and spend the night somewhere in America."

Another real barrier to our taking any part in the war was our sincere, profound, traditional love of peace. This does not mean, of course, that America is a country of pacifists. Our history proves the contrary. Our conscientious objections to certain shameful things, like injustice, and dishonor, and tyranny, and systematic cruelty, are stronger than our conscientious objection to fighting. But our national policy is averse to war, and our national institutions are not favorable to its sudden declaration or swift prosecution.

In effect, the United States is a pacific nation of fighting men.

What was it, then, that forced such a nation into a conflict of arms?

It was the growing sense that the very existence of this war was a crime against humanity, that it need not and ought not to have been begun, and that the only way to put a stop to it was to join the Allies, who had tried to prevent its beginning, and who are still trying to bring it to the only end that will be a finality.

It was also the conviction that the Monroe Doctrine, so far from being an obstacle, was an incentive to our entrance. The real basis of that doctrine is the right of free peoples, however small and weak, to maintain by common consent their own forms of government. This Germany and Austria denied. The issue at stake was no longer merely European. It was worldwide.

The Monroe Doctrine could not be saved in one continent if its foundation was destroyed in another. The only way to save it was to broaden it.

The United States, having grown to be a World Power, must either uphold everywhere the principles by which it had been begotten and made great or sink into the state of an obese, helpless parasite. Its sister republics would share its fate.

But more than this: it was the flagrant and contemptuous disregard of all the principles of international law and common humanity by the Imperial German Government that alarmed and incensed us. The list of crimes and atrocities ordered in this war by the mysterious and awful power that rules the German people-- which I prefer to call, for the sake of brevity and impersonality, the Potsdam gang-- is too long to be repeated here. The levying of unlawful tribute from captured cities and villages; the use of old men, women, and children as a screen for advancing troops; the extortion of military information from civilians by cruel and barbarous methods; the burning and destruction of entire towns as a punishment for the actual or suspected hostile deeds of individuals, and the brutal avowal that in this punishment it was necessary that "the innocent shall suffer with the guilty" (see the letter of General von Nieber to the burgomaster of Wavre, August 27, and the proclamation of Governor-General von der Goltz, September 2, 1914); the introduction of the use of asphyxiating gas as a weapon of war (at Ypres, April 22, 1915); the poisoning of wells; the reckless and needless destruction of priceless monuments of art like the Cathedral of Reims; the deliberate and treacherous violation of the Red Cross, which is the sign of mercy and compassion for all Christendom; the bombardment of hospitals and the cold-blooded slaughter of nurses and wounded men; the sinking of hospital ships with their helpless and suffering company--all these, and many other infamies committed by order of the Potsdam gang made the heart of America hot and angry against the power which devised and commanded such brutality. True, they were not, technically speaking, crimes directed against the United States. They did not injure our material interests. They injured only our souls and the world in which we have to live. They were vivid illustrations of the inward nature of that German Kultur whose superiority, the German professors say, "is rooted in the unfathomable depths of its moral constitution." (Deutsche Reden in Schwerer Zeit, II, p. 23.)

But there were two criminal blunders--or perhaps it would be more accurate to call them two series of obstinate and stupid offenses against international law-- by which the Potsdam gang directly assailed the sovereignty and neutrality of the United States and forced us to choose between the surrender of our national integrity and a frank acceptance of the war which Germany was waging, not only against our principles and interests, but against the things which in our judgment were essential to the welfare of mankind and to the existence of honorable and decent relations among the peoples of the world.

The first of these offenses was the cynical and persistent attempt to take advantage of the good nature and unsuspiciousness of the United States for the establishment of an impudent system of German espionage; to use our territory as a base of conspiracy and treacherous hostilities against countries with which we were at peace; and to lose no opportunity of mobilizing the privileges granted by "these idiotic Yankees" (quotation from the military attache of the Imperial German Embassy at Washington)--including, of course, the diplomatic privilege--to make America unconsciously help in playing the game of the Potsdam gang.

The second of these offenses was the illegal, piratical submarine warfare which the Potsdam gang ordered and waged against the merchant shipping of the world, thereby destroying the lives and the property of American citizens and violating the most vital principle of our steadfast contention for the freedom of the sea.

The message of the President to Congress on April 2, 1917, marked these two offenses as the main causes which made it impossible for the United States to maintain longer an official attitude of neutrality toward the German Government, which "did what it pleased and told its people nothing." The President generously declared that the source of these offenses "lay not in any hostile feeling or purpose of the German people toward us." That was a magnanimous declaration, and we sincerely hope it may prove true.

But practically the difficulty lies in the fact that at the present hour several millions of the German people stand in arms, on land that does not belong to them, to maintain the purpose and continue the practices of the Potsdam gang. It is a pity, but it is true. The only way to get at the gang which chose and forced this atrocious war is to go through the armed people who still defend that choice and the atrocities which have emphasized it.

Forgiveness must wait upon repentance. Repentance must be proved by restitution and reparation. Any other settlement of this world conflict would be a world calamity. For America and for all the Allies who are fighting for a peace worth having and keeping, the watchword must be: Stand fast, ye free!

II

The offenses against the neutrality of the United States which were instigated and financed by the Potsdam gang were enumerated by the Committee on Foreign Affairs of the House of Representatives in the first week of April, 1917, and amounted to at least twenty-one distinct crimes or unfriendly acts, including the furnishing of bogus passports to German reservists and spies, the incitement of rebellion in India and in Mexico, the preparation of dynamite outrages against Canada, the placing of bombs in ships sailing from American ports, and many other ill-judged pleasantries of a similar character.

The crown was put on this series of blundering misdeeds by the note of January 19, 1917, sent from the German Foreign Office (under cover of our diplomatic privilege, of course) to the German Minister in Mexico, directing him to prepare an alliance with that country against the United States in the event of war, urging him to use Mexico as an agent to draw Japan into that alliance, and offering as a bribe to the Mexicans the possession of American territory in Texas, New Mexico, and Arizona. (See War Message and Facts Behind It, p. 13. Published by the Committee on Public Information, Washington, Government Printing Office, 1917.)

The fact is, we have only just begun to understand the real nature of the German secret service, which works with, and either under or over, the diplomatic service.

It is certainly the most highly organized, systematic, and expensive, and at the same time probably the most bone-headed and unscrupulous, secret service in the world.

Its powers of falsification and evasion are only exceeded by its capacity for making those mistakes which spring from a congenital contempt for other people.

At The Hague I had numerous opportunities of observing and noting the workings of this peculiar system. The story of many of them cannot be publicly told without violating that reserve which I prefer to maintain in regard to confidential communications and private affairs in which the personal reputation of individuals is involved. But there are two or three experiences of which I may write freely without incurring either self-reproach or a just reproach from others. They are not at all sensational. But they seemed at the time, and they seem still, to have a certain significance as indications of the psychology of the people with whom we were then in nominal friendship.

Three requests were made to me for the forwarding of important communications to Brussels under cover of the diplomatic privilege of the American Legation. The memoranda of the dates and so on are in the Chancellery at The Hague, so I cannot refer to them. But it is certain that the requests came shortly after the beginning of the war, in the first or second week of August, 1914, and the content and purport of them are absolutely clear in my memory.

The first request was from Berlin for the transmission of a note to the Belgian Government, renewing the proposition which the Potsdam gang had made on August 2: namely, that Belgium should permit the free passage of German troops through her neutral ground on condition that Germany would pay for all damage done and that Belgian territory would not be annexed. (Off. Dip. Doc., p. 402.) King Albert had already replied, on August 3, to this proposition, saying that to permit such a passage of hostile troops against France would be "a flagrant violation of international law" and would "sacrifice the honor of the nation." (Off. Dip. Doc., p. 421.) After such an answer it did not seem to me that the renewal of the dishonorable proposal was likely to have a good effect. Yet the Berlin note was entirely correct in form. It merely offered a chance for Belgium to choose again between peace with the friendship of Germany and dishonor attached, and war in defense of the neutrality to which she was bound by the very treaties (1831, 1839) which brought her into being. I had no right to interpose an obstacle to the repetition of Belgium's first heroic choice. I pointed out that, not being accredited to the Belgian Government, I was not in a position to transmit any communication to it. But I was willing to forward the note to my colleague the American Minister in Brussels, absolutely without recommendation, but simply for such disposal as he thought fit. Accordingly the note was transmitted to him.[7]

What Whitlock did with it I do not know. What answer, if any, Belgium made I do not know. But I do know that she stood to her guns and kept her honor intact and immortal.

The second request was of a different quality. It came to me from the Imperial German Legation at The Hague. It was a note for transmission to the Belgian Government, beginning with a reference to the fall of Liege and the hopeless folly of attempting to resist the German invasion, and continuing with an intimation of the terrible consequences which would follow Belgium's persistence in her mad idea of keeping her word of honor. In effect the note was a curious combination of an insult and a threat. I promptly and positively refused to transmit it or to have anything to do with it.

"But why," said the German counsellor, sitting by my study fire---a Prussian of the Prussians--"why do you refuse? You are a neutral, a friend of both parties. Why not simply transmit the note to your colleague in Brussels as you did before? You are not in any way responsible for its contents."

"Quite so," I answered, "and thank God for that! But suppose you had a quarrel with a neighbor in the Rheinland, who had positively declined a proposition which you had made to him. And suppose, the ordinary post-boy services being interrupted, you asked me to convey to your neighbor a note which began by addressing him as a 'silly s-- of a b----,' and ended by telling him that if he did not agree you would certainly grind him to powder. Would you expect me to play the post-boy for such a billet-doux on the ground that I was not responsible for its contents and was a friend of both parties?"

"Well," replied the counsellor, laughing at the North American directness of my language, "probably not." So he folded up the note and took it away. What became of it I do not know nor care.

The third request was of still another quality. It came from the Imperial Austro-Hungarian Legation, which very politely asked me to transmit a message in the American diplomatic code to my colleague in Brussels for delivery to the Austro-Hungarian Legation, which still lingered in that city. The first and last parts of the

7   My colleague, Honorable James W. Gerard, Ex-Ambassador to Germany, has referred to this in his very interesting book, "My Four Years in Germany," p. 136.

message were in plain language, good English, quite innocent and proper. But the kernel of the despatch was written in the numerical secret cipher of Vienna, which of course I was unable to read. I drew attention to this, and asked mildly how I could be expected to put this passage into our code without knowing what the words were. The answer was that it would not be necessary to code this passage; it could be transmitted in numbers just as it stood; the Austro-Hungarian charge d'affaires at Brussels would understand it.

"Quite so," I answered, "but you see the point is that I do not understand it. My dear count, you are my very good friend, and it grieves me deeply to decline any requests of yours. But the simple fact is that our instructions explicitly forbid us to send any message in two codes."

The count--who, by the way, was an excellent and most amiable man-- blushed and stammered that he was only carrying out the instructions of his chief, but that my point was perfectly clear and indisputable. I was glad that he saw it in that light, and we parted on the most friendly terms. What became of the message I do not know nor care.

It was about the 1st of September, 1915, that I came into brief contact with the case of Mr. J. F. J. Archibald. This gentleman was an American journalist, and a very clever and agreeable man. We had met some months before, when he was on his way back to America from his professional work in Germany, and he had been a welcome guest at my table. But the second meeting was different.

This time Mr. Archibald was returning toward Germany on the Holland-America steamship Rotterdam. When the boat touched at Falmouth, on August 30, the British authorities examined his luggage and found that he was carrying private letters and official despatches from Doctor Dumba the Austrian Ambassador at Washington, from Count Bernstorff the German Ambassador, and from Captain von Papen his military attache. Not only was the carrying of these letters by a private person on a regular mail route a recognized offense against the law, but the documents themselves contained matter of an incriminating and seditious nature, most unfriendly to the United States. The egregious Doctor Dumba, for example, described how it would be possible to "disorganize and hold up for months if not entirely prevent," the work of American factories; and the colossal Captain von Papen, in a letter referring to the activities of German secret agents in America, gave birth to his eloquent and unforgettable phrase, "these idiotic Yankees." The papers, of course, were taken from Mr. Archibald at Falmouth, but he was allowed to continue his voyage to Rotterdam en route for Berlin.

Before his arrival, however, a cablegram came from the Department of State at Washington instructing me to take up his regular passport which was made out to cover travel in Germany; to give him an emergency passport valid for one month and good only for the return to the United States; and to use all proper means to get him back to New York at the earliest possible date.

Having found out that he was lodged at a certain hotel I sent him a courteous invitation to call at the Legation on business of importance. He came promptly and we sat down in the library for a conversation which you will admit had its delicate points.

He began by saying that he supposed I had seen the newspaper accounts of what happened to him at Falmouth; that he was greatly surprised and chagrined about the matter; that he had been entirely ignorant of the contents of the documents found in his possession; that he had imagined--indeed he had been distinctly told--that they were innocent private letters relating to personal and domestic affairs; that he did not know there was any impropriety in conveying such letters; that if he had suspected their nature or known that they included official despatches he would never have taken them.

I replied that his personal statement was enough for me on that point, but that it seemed to throw rather a dark shadow on the character and conduct of his friends in the German and Austrian Embassies who had knowingly exposed his innocence to such a risk. I added that it was probably with a view to obtaining his help in clearing up the matter that the Department of State had instructed me to take up his passport.

"But have you the legal right to do that?"

"Under American law, yes, unquestionably."

"But under Dutch law?"

"Probably not. But I hope it will not be necessary to invoke that law. Simply to inform the Dutch Foreign Minister of the presence of an American whose passport had been revoked but who refused to give it up, would be sufficient for my purpose."

He reflected for a moment, and then said, smiling:

"I don't refuse to give it up. Here it is. Now tell me what I shall do without a passport.

"Thank you. Fortunately I have authority to give you an emergency passport, good for a month, and covering the return voyage to America."

"But I don't want to go there. I want to go on to Berlin."

"Unfortunately I fear that will be impossible. Your old passport is invalid and will not carry you over the Dutch border. Your new passport cannot be made out for Germany. Your best course is to return home."

"I see. But have you any right to arrest me and send me to America?"

"None whatever, my dear sir. Please don't misunderstand me. This is just a bit of friendly advice. 'Your country needs you.' You naturally want an early chance to tell Washington what you have told me. The Rotterdam is a very comfortable ship, and she sails for New York the day after to-morrow. I have already bespoken an excellent room for you. Do you accept?"

"Yes, and thank you for the way you have put the matter. But do you think they will arrest me when I get to New York?"

"Probably not. But to help in forestalling that unpleasant possibility I will cable Washington that you are coming at once, of your own free will, and anxious to tell the whole story."

So he went, and I saw him off on the Rotterdam, a pallid and downcast figure. I pitied him. It seemed strange that any one should ever trust that unscrupulous, callous, thick-pated diplomatic-secret-service machine which is always ready to expose a too confiding and admiring friend to danger or disgrace in order to serve its imperious necessities.

Holland, of course, owing to its geographical situation, was a regular nest of German espionage. Other spies were there, too, but they were much less in evidence than the Germans. Of the tricks and the manners of the latter I had some picturesque experiences which I do not feel at liberty to narrate. The Department of State has been informed of them, and has no doubt put the information safely away with a lot of other things which it knows but does not think it expedient or necessary to tell until the proper time.

But there is no reason why the simple little tale of the futile attempt to plant two German spies in my household at The Hague should not be told. One of the men in our domestic service, a Hollander, had been obliged to leave and we wanted to fill his place. This was difficult because the requirements of the Dutch army service claimed such a large number of the younger men.

The first who applied for the vacant place professed to be a Belgian. Perhaps he was. On demand he produced his "papers"--birth-certificate, baptismal registry, several Passier-scheine, and so forth. But down in a corner on the back of one of the papers was a dim blue stamp--"Imperial German Marine." What was the meaning of this? What had the Potsdam High-Sea Fleet to do with this peaceable overland traveller from Belgium? Voluble excuses, but no satisfactory explanation. I told him that I feared he was too experienced for the place.

The second who applied was an unquestionable Dutchman, young, good- looking, intelligent. Papers in perfect order. Present service with a well-known pro-German family. Previous service of one year with a lady who was one of my best friends--the wife of a high government official. I rang her up on the telephone and asked if she could tell me anything about A. B., who had been in service with her for a year. A second of silence, then the answer: "Yes, a good deal, but not on the telephone, please. Come around to tea this afternoon." Madame L. then told me that while the young man was clean, sober, and industrious, he had been found rummaging among her husband's official papers, in a room which he was forbidden to enter, and had been caught several times listening at the keyhole of doors while private conferences were going on.

It seemed to me that a young man with such an uncontrollable thirst for knowledge would not be suited for the very simple service which would be required of him in our household.

Afterward, traces of both of these men were found which led unmistakably to the lair of the chief spider of the German secret service at The Hague. The incident was a very small one. But, after all, life is made up of small incidents with a connected meaning.

At the time when I am writing this (September 24, 1917) the moral character of the tools of the Potsdam gang has again been stripped naked by the disclosure of the treachery by which the German Legation in Argentina has utilized the Swedish Legation in that country to transmit, under diplomatic privilege, messages inciting to murder on the high seas. Argentina has already taken the action to be expected from an American Republic by dismissing the German Minister. What Sweden will do to vindicate her honor remains to be seen. Her attitude may affect our opinion of her as a victim or a vassal of Potsdam.

There are two points in the disclosures made on September 23 by the Department of State which bear directly upon this simple narrative of experiences at The Hague.

The fetching female comic-opera star, Ray Beveridge, discreetly alluded to in the third chapter (p. 71), was secretly paid three thousand dollars by the Imperial German Embassy in Washington to finance her artistic activities. So, you see, I was not far wrong in forwarding her divorce papers to Germany and refusing to transmit her newspaper correspondence to America. She was a paid soubrette in the Potsdam troupe.

The affable and intelligent Mr. Archibald, alluded to in this chapter (p. 169), received on April 21, 1915, according to these disclosures, five thousand dollars from the Imperial German Embassy in Washington for "propaganda" services. If I had known this when he came to me in September, it is possible that I should have been less careful to spare his feelings.

III

The record of the German submarine warfare on merchant shipping is one of the most extraordinary chapters in history. Americans have read it with appropriate indignation, but not always with clear understanding of the precise issues involved. Let me try to make those issues plain, since the submarine campaign was one of the causes which forced this war upon the United States. (President's Message to Congress, April 2, 1917, paragraphs 2-10.)

In war all naval vessels, including of course submarines, have the right to attack and destroy, by any means in their power, any war-ship of the enemy. In regard to merchant-ships the case is different, according to international law. (See G. G. Wilson, International Law, paragraphs 114, 136, New York, 1901-1909.)

The war-vessel has the right of "visit and search" on all merchant-ships, enemy or neutral. It has also the right, in case the cargo of the merchant-ship appears to include more than a certain percentage of contraband, to capture it and take it into a port for adjudication as a prize. The war-vessel has also the right to sink a presumptive prize under conditions (such as distance, stress of weather, and so forth) which make it impossible to take it into port.

But here the right of the war-vessel stops. It has absolutely no right to sink the merchant-ship without warning and without making efficient provision for the safety of the passengers and crew. That is the common law of civilized nations. To break it is to put one's self beyond the pale.

Some Germanophile critics have faulted me for calling the Teutonic submarines "Potsdam pirates." A commissioned vessel, these critics say, which merely executes the orders of its government, cannot properly be called a pirate.

Why not? Take the definition of piracy given in the New Oxford Dictionary: "The crime of robbery or depredation on the sea by persons not holding a commission from an established civilized state."

There's the point! Is a nation which orders its servants to commit deeds forbidden by international law, a nation which commands its naval officers to commit deliberate, wanton, dastardly murder on the high seas (case of Belgian Prince, July 31, 1917, and others), is such a nation to be regarded as "an established civilized state"?

Were Algiers and Tunis and Tripoli "civilized states" when they sent out the Barbary pirates in the eighteenth and early nineteenth centuries? We thought not, and we sent our war-ships to whip the barbarism out of them.

Commodore Stephen Decatur, in 1815, forced the cruel and cowardly Dey of Algiers to sign a deed of renunciation and a promise of good conduct, on the deck of an American frigate, under the Stars and Stripes.

A hundred years ago the glory of the American navy was made clear to the world in the suppression of the pirates of North Africa. To-day that glory must be maintained by firm, fearless, unrelenting war against the pirates of North Germany.

A commission to do a certain thing which is in itself unlawful does not change the nature of the misdeed. No nation has a right to commission its officers to violate the law of nations.

But the Germans say their submarines are such wonderful, delicate, scientific machines that it is impossible for them to give warning of an attack, or to do anything to save the helpless people whose peaceful vessel has been sunk beneath their feet. The precious, fragile submarine cannot be expected to observe any law of humanity which would imperil its further usefulness as an instrument of destruction.

Marvellous argument--worthy of the Potsdam mind in its highest state of Kultur! By the same reasoning any assassin might claim the right to kill without resistance because he proposed to commit the crime with a dagger so delicately wrought, so frail, so slender, that the slightest struggle on the part of his victim would break the costly, beautiful, murderous weapon.

Again, these extraordinary Germans say that merchant-ships ought not to carry weapons for defense; it is too dangerous for the dainty U-boat; every merchantman thus armed must be treated as a vessel of war. But the law of nations for more than two centuries has sanctioned the carrying of defensive armament by merchant-ships, and precisely because they might need it to protect themselves against pirates.

Shall the United States be asked to rewrite this article of international law, in the midst of a great war on sea and land? Shall the government at Washington be seduced by cajolery, or compelled by threats, to rob the merchantmen of the poor protection of a single gun in order that they may fall absolutely helpless into the black hands of the prowling Potsdam pirates? That would be neutrality with a vengeance! Yet that is just what the Imperial German Government tried to persuade or force the United States to do. Thank God the effort was vain.

These were the matters under discussion when I was called to Washington in February, 1916, for consultation with the President. The long and wearing controversy had been going on for months. Every month notes were coming from Berlin, each more evasive and unsatisfactory than the last. Every week Count Bernstorff and his aides were coming to the State Department with new excuses, new subterfuges, and the same old lies. The President and Secretary Lansing, both of whom are excellent international lawyers, found their patience tried to the uttermost by the absurdity of the arguments presented to them and by the veiled contempt in the manner of the presentation. But they kept their tempers and did their best to keep the peace.

On two points they were firm as adamant. First, the law of nations should not and could not be changed in the midst of a war to suit the need of one of the parties. Second, "the use of submarines for the destruction of commerce is of necessity, because of the very character of the vessels employed and the very methods of attack which their employment of course involves, incompatible with the principles of humanity, the long-established and incontrovertible rights of neutrals, and the sacred immunities of non-combatants." (President Wilson's Address to Congress, April 19, 1916.)

It was on my return from this visit to Washington that I had an opportunity of observing at close range the crooked methods of the Potsdam gang in regard to the U-boat warfare. Arriving at The Hague on March 24, 1916, I found Holland aflame with helpless rage over the recent sinking of the S.S. Tubantia, the newest and best boat of the Netherlands-Lloyd merchant-fleet. She was torpedoed by an unseen submarine on March 15.

An explanation was promptly demanded from the German Government, which denied any knowledge of the affair. Holland, lacking evidence as to the perpetrator of the crime, would have had to swallow this denial but for an accident which furnished her with the missing proof. One of the Tubantia's small boats drifted ashore. In the boat was a fragment of a Schwarzkopf torpedo--a type manufactured and used only by Germany. This fragment was forwarded to Berlin, with another and more urgent demand for explanation, apology, and reparation.

The German newspapers coolly replied with the astounding statement that there had been two or three Schwarzkopf torpedoes in naval museums in England, and that this particular specimen had probably been given to a British submarine and used by her to destroy the good ship Tubantia.

Again Holland would have been left helpless, choking with indignation, but for a second accident. Another of the lost steamship's boats was found, and in it there was another fragment of the torpedo. This fragment bore the mark of the German navy, telling just when the torpedo was made and to which of the U-boats it had been issued.

With this bit of damning evidence in his bag a Dutch naval expert was sent to Berlin to get to the bottom of the crime and to demand justice. He got there, but he found no justice in that shop.

The German navy is very systematic, keeps accurate books, makes no accidental mistake. The pedigree and record of the Schwarzkopf were found. It was issued to a certain U-boat on a certain date. Undoubtedly it was the missile which unfortunately sank the Tubantia. All this was admitted and deeply regretted. But Germany was free from all responsibility for the sad occurrence. The following amazing reason was given by the Imperial German Government.

This certain U-boat had fired this certain torpedo at a British war-vessel somewhere in the North Sea ten days before the Tubantia was sunk. The shot missed its mark. But the naughty, undisciplined little torpedo went cruising around in the sea on its own hook for ten days waiting for a chance to kill somebody. Then the Tubantia came along, and the wandering-Willy torpedo promptly, stupidly, ran into the ship and sank her. This was the explanation. Germany was not to blame. (See the official report in the Orange Books of the Netherlands Government, July, 1916, December, 1916.)

This stupendous fairy-tale Holland was expected to believe and to accept as the end of the affair. She did not believe it. She had to accept it. What else could she do? Fight? She did not want to share Belgium's dreadful fate. The Dutch Government proposed that the whole Tubantia incident be submitted to an international commission. The German Government accepted this proposal en principe, but said it must be deferred until after the war.

I wonder why some of the Americans who blame Holland for not being in arms against Germany never think of that stern and awful deterrent which stands under her eyes and presses upon her very bosom. She is still independent, still neutral, still unravaged. Five-sixths of her people, I believe, have no sympathy with the German Government in its choice and conduct of this war. At least this was the case while I was at The Hague. But the one thing that Holland is, above all else, is pro-Dutch. She wants to keep her liberty, her sovereignty, her land untouched. To defend these treasures she will fight, and for no other reason. I have heard Queen Wilhelmina say this a score of times. She means it, and her people are with her.

Seven Dutch ships were sunk in a bunch in the English Channel by the Potsdam pirates on February 22, 1917. Holland was furious. She stated her grievance, protested, remonstrated--and there she stopped. If she had tried to do anything more she stood to lose a third of her territory in a few days and the whole in a few weeks--lose it, mark you, to the gang that ruined Belgium.

But the position, and therefore the case, of America in regard to the German submarine warfare was quite different. She was one of the eight "Big Powers" of the world. She was the mightiest of the neutrals.

Her rights at sea were no greater than theirs. But her duties were greater, just because she was larger, more powerful, better able to champion those rights not only for herself but also for others.

She would not have to pay such an instant, awful, crushing penalty for armed resistance to the brutalities of the Potsdam gang as would certainly be inflicted upon the little northern neutrals if they attempted to defend themselves against injustice and aggression.

Their part was to make protest, and record it, and wait for justice until the war was ended. America's part was to make protest, and then--her protest being mocked, scorned, disregarded--to stand up in arms with France and Great Britain and help to end the war by a victory of righteous peace.

But did we not also have objections to some of the measures and actions of the British blockade--as, for instance, the seizure and search of the mails? Certainly we did, and Secretary Lansing stated them clearly and maintained them firmly. But here is the difference. These objections concerned only the rights of neutral property on the high seas. We knew by positive assurance from England, and by our experience with her in the Alabama Claims Arbitration, that she was ready to refer all such questions to an impartial tribunal and abide by its decision. Our objections to the conduct of the German navy concerned the far more sacred rights of "life, liberty, and the pursuit of happiness."

The murder of one American child at sea meant more to us than the seizure of a thousand cargoes of alleged contraband.

No one has ever accused the British or French or Italian sailors in this war of sinking merchant-ships without warning, leaving their crews and passengers to drown. On the contrary, British seamen have risked and lost their lives in a chivalrous attempt to save the lives even of their enemies after the fair sinking of a German war-ship.

But the hands of the Potsdam pirates are red with innocent blood. The bottom of the sea is strewn with the wrecks they have made. "The dark unfathom'd caves of ocean" hide the bones of their helpless victims, who shall arise at the judgment-day to testify against them.

On May 7, 1915, the passenger liner Lusitania, unarmed, was sunk without warning by a German U-boat off the Irish coast. One hundred and fourteen Americans--men, women, and little children, lawful and peaceful travellers--were drowned--

"Butchered to make a [German] holiday."

The holiday was celebrated in Germany. The schools were let out. The soldiers in the reserve camps had leave to join in the festivities. The towns and cities were filled with fluttering flags and singing folks. A German pastor preached: "Whoever cannot bring himself to approve from the bottom of his heart the sinking of the Lusitania--him we judge to be no true German." (Deutsche Reden in Schwerer Zeit, No. 24, p. 7.) A medal was struck to commemorate the great achievement. It is a very ugly medal. I keep a copy of it in order that I may never forget the character of a nation which was not content with rejoicing over such a crime but desired to immortalize it in bronze.

The three strong and eloquent notes of President Wilson in regard to the Lusitania are too well known to be quoted here. The practical answer from Potsdam (passing over the usual subterfuges and falsehoods) was the sinking of the Arabic August 19 and the murder of three more Americans. Then the correspondence languished until the torpedoing (March 24, 1916) of the Sussex, a Channel ferry-boat, crowded with passengers, among whom were many Americans. Then the President sent a flat message calling down the Potsdam pirates and declaring that unless they abandoned their nefarious practices "the United States had no choice but to sever diplomatic relations with the German Empire altogether" (April 18, 1916).

This brought a grudging promise from Germany that she would henceforth refrain from sinking merchant-vessels "without warning and without saving human lives, unless the ship attempted to escape or offer resistance." How this promise was kept may be judged from the sinking of the Marina (October 28), with the loss of eight American lives, and of the Russian (December 14), with the loss of seventeen American lives, and other similar sinkings.

During all this time Germany had been building new and larger submarines with wonderful industry. She had filled up her pack of sea-wolves. On January 31, 1917, she revoked her flimsy pledge, let loose her wolf-pack, and sent word to all the neutral nations that she would sink at sight all ships found in the zones which she had marked "around Great Britain, France, Italy, and in the Eastern Mediterranean." (Why We Are at War, p. 23, New York, 1917.) The President promptly broke off diplomatic relations (February 3), and said that we should refrain from hostilities until the commission of "actual overt acts" by Germany forced us to the conviction that she meant to carry out her base threat.

The overt acts came quickly. Between February 3 and April 1 eight American merchant-ships were sunk, and more than forty American lives were destroyed by the Potsdam pirates.

The die was cast. On April 2, 1917, the President advised Congress that the United States could no longer delay the formal acceptance of "the status of belligerent which had been thrust upon it." On April 6 Congress took the necessary action. On the same day the President proclaimed that "a state of war exists between the United States and the Imperial German Government."

Back of this momentous and noble decision, in which the hearts of the immense majority of Americans are with the President, there are undoubtedly many strong and righteous reasons. Some of these I have tried to set forth in the first part of this article. But we must never forget that the specific reason given by the President, the definite cause which forced us into the war, is the German method of submarine warfare, which he has repeatedly denounced as illegal, immoral, inhuman--a direct and brutal attack upon us and upon all mankind. These words cannot be forgotten, nor is it likely that the President will retract them.

They set up at least one steadfast mark in the midst of the present flood of peace talk. There can be no parley with a criminal who is in full and exultant practice of his crime. Unless the U-boat warfare is renounced, repented of, and abandoned by the Potsdam pirates, an honorable peace is unattainable except by fighting for it and winning it.[8]

IV

Only a little space is left for writing of my retirement from the post at The Hague and my experiences thereafter in England and France.

The reader may have gathered from the tenor of these chapters that the work at the legation was hard and that the situation was trying to a man with strong convictions and the habit of expressing them frankly. My resignation was tendered in September, 1916, with the request that it should not be made public until after the re-election of President Wilson, which I earnestly desired and expected. My reasons for resigning were partly of a domestic nature. But the main reason was a personal wish to get back to my work as a writer, "with full freedom to say what I thought and felt about the war."

The German-American press has tried to start a rumor that I was recalled to Washington to explain my action on a certain point. That is absolutely and entirely false. The government never asked for an explanation of anything in my conduct while in office, or afterward. On the contrary, the President has been kind enough to express his approval of my services in terms too friendly to be quoted here.

In November, after President Wilson had been triumphantly chosen for a second term, I ventured to recall his attention to my letter of September. He answered that he would "reluctantly yield" to my wishes, but would appreciate my remaining at The Hague until a successor could be found for the post. Of course I willingly agreed to this.

In December the name of this successor was cabled to me with instructions to find out whether he would be acceptable to the Queen and the Government of Hol-

---

8   Belgian Relief ships sunk: S.S. Camilla, Trevier, Feistein, Storstad, Lars Kruse, Euphrates. Haelen, and Tunis (the last two shelled but not sunk).

Hospital ships sunk: Britannic (probably but not certainly torpedoed); Asturias, March 24. 1917; Gloucester Castle, March 30; Donegal, April 17; Lanfranc, April 17 (with British wounded and German wounded prisoners).

Among the neutral nations Norway alone has lost more than six hundred ships by mines and torpedoes of German origin. The dance of death still goes on.

land. Her Majesty said that this gentleman would certainly be persona grata, and I cabled to Washington to this effect.

Early in January a message came from the Secretary of State saying that, as all was arranged except the final confirmation of the appointment, I might feel free to leave at my convenience. Having cleaned up my work and left everything in order for my successor (including the lease of my house), I took ship from Flushing for England on January 15, 1917.

The voyage through the danger zone was uneventful. The visit to England was unforgettable.

Everywhere I saw the evidences that Great Britain was at war, in earnest, and resolved to "carry on" with her Allies until the victory of a real peace was won.

Women and girls were at work in the railway stations, on the trams and omnibuses, in the munition factories, in postal and telegraph service, doing the tasks of men. We shall have to revise that phrase which speaks of "the weaker sex."

By night London was

"Dark, dark, dark, irrecoverably dark."

But it was not still, nor terrified by the instant danger of Zeppelin raids. Every time a German vulture passed over England dropping bolts of indiscriminate death, it woke the heart of the people to a new impulse, not of fear but of hot indignation.

By day the great city swarmed with eager life. Business was going on at full swing, though not "as usual." Women were driving trucks, carrying packages, running ticket-offices. Men in khaki outnumbered those in civilian dress. Wounded soldiers hobbled cheerfully along the streets. The parks were adorned with hospitals. Mrs. Pankhurst spoke from a soap-box near the Marble Arch; not now for woman-suffrage--"That will come," she said, "but the great thing to-day is to carry on the war to a victory for freedom!"

Oxford--gray city of the golden dream, Learning's fairest and most lovely seat in all the world--Oxford was transformed into a hospital for the wounded, a training-camp for new soldiers, a nursery of noble manhood equipped for the stern duties of war.

Every family that I knew was in grief for a dear one lost on the field of glorious strife. But not one was in mourning. The great sacrifice was bravely accepted as a part of the greater duty.

The friends with whom I talked most--men like Lord Bryce, Sir Sydney Lee, Sir Herbert Warren, Sir Robertson Nicoll, Sir William Osler--were lovers of peace, tried and well-known. All were of one mind in holding that Britain's faith and honor bound her to accept the war when Germany violated Belgium, and that it must be fought through until the Prussian military autocracy which began it was broken.

There were restricted rations in England; but no starvation and no sign of it. There were partisan criticisms and plenty of "grousing." The Britisher is never contented unless he can grumble--especially at his own government. But there was no lack of a real unity of purpose, nor of a solid, cheerful, bull-dog determination to hang on to the enemy until he came down. It is this spirit that has enabled a nation, which was almost ignorant of what military preparedness meant, to put between three and four million troops into the field in defense of justice and liberty.

At the end of January I went to France, eager to see with my own eyes the great things that were doing there and to taste with my own lips the cup of danger. That at least I was bound to do before I could come home and urge my countrymen to face the duty and brave the peril of a part in this war.

Paris was not so dark as London but more tragic. After Belgium and Servia the heaviest brunt of this dreadful conflict has fallen upon France. She has suffered most. Yet on the faces of her women I saw no tears and in the eyes of her men no fear nor regret.

If Britain was magnificent, France was miraculous! Loving and desiring peace she accepted the cross of war without a murmur. Her women were no less brave than her men. She wears the hero-star of Roland and the saintly halo of Joan of Arc.

After meeting many men in Paris--statesmen, men of letters, generals--and after visiting the splendid American Ambulance at Neuilly and other institutions in which our boys and girls were giving their help to France in the chivalric spirit of Lafayette, I went out toward the front.

The first visit was under the escort of Captain Francois Monod to a chateau beyond Compiegne, where Rudyard Kipling with his family and I with my family had passed the Christmas week of 1913 together, as joyous guests of the American chatelaine Mrs. Julia Park. She has given the spacious, lovely house for a military hospital. And there, while the German guns thundered a few kilometres away from us and a German sausage balloon floated in the sky, I watched the skilful ministrations of French and American doctors and nurses to the wounded.

One thought haunted me--the memory of Kipling's only son, nineteen years old, who was with us in that happy Christmastide. The lad was reported "missing" after one of the battles between Loos and Hulluch. For six months I sought, with the help of Herr von Kuhlmann, German Minister at The Hague, to find a trace of the brave boy. But never a word could we get.

The second visit was to the battle-field of the Marne under the escort of Captain the Count de Ganay. We motored slowly through the ruined towns and villages. Those which had been wrecked by shellfire were like mouthfuls of broken teeth--chimneys and fragments of walls still standing. Those which had been vengefully burned by the retreating Germans were mere heaps of ashes. Most of our time was spent around the Marais de St. Gond, where the French General Foch held the Thermopylae of Europe.

Four times he advanced across that marsh and was driven back, but not beaten. The fifth time he advanced and stayed, and Paris was forever lost to the Germans. Think of the men who made that last advance and saved Europe from the Potsdam gang. Their graves, carefully marked and tended, lie thickly strewn along the lonely ridges of all that region--humble but immortal reminders of glorious heroism.

The third visit was with the same escort to the fighting front at Verdun.

The long, bare, rolling ridges between Bar-le-Duc and the Meuse; the high-shouldered hills along the river and around the ruined little city; the open fields, the narrow valleys, the wrecked villages, the shattered woodlands--all were covered with dazzling snow. The sun was bright in a cloudless sky. A bitter, biting wind poured fiercely, steadily out of the north, driving the glittering snow-dust before it. Every man had put on all the clothes he possessed, and more; pads of sheepskin over back and breast; gunny sacks tied around the shoulders. The troops of cavalry, the teams of mules and horses dragging munition-wagons or travelling kitchens or long "75" guns, clattered along the iron surface of the Via Sacra--that blessed road which made the salvation of Verdun possible after the only railway was destroyed. Endless trains of motor-lorries lumbered by. The narrow trenches were coated with ice. The hillside trails were slippery as glass. In the deep dugouts small sheet-iron stoves were burning, giving out a little heat and a great deal of choking smoke. The soldiers sat around them playing cards or telling stories.

But there! What I saw in that shell-pitted, snow-covered, hard-frozen amphitheatre of heroism cannot be described in these brief paragraphs. The serenity, cheerfulness, courtesy, and indomitable courage of the French poilus defending their own land; the scenes in the trenches with the German shells breaking around us and the wounded men being carried past us; the luncheon in the citadel with the commandant and officers in a subterranean room where the motto on the wall, above the world-renowned escutcheon of Verdun, was "On ne passe pas"--"They don't get by"; the dinner with the general and staff of the Verdun army, in a little village "somewhere in France," and their last words to me, "On les aura! Ca peut etre long, mais on les aura!"--"It may take long, but we shall get them!"--all these and a thousand more things are vivid in my memory but cannot be told now.

One scene sticks in my mind and asks to be recorded.

The hospital was just back of the Verdun lines. Its roofs were marked with the Red Cross. Twenty-four hundred beds, all clean and quiet. Wards full of German wounded, cared for as tenderly as the French. "Will you see an operation?" said the proud little commandant who was showing me through his domain. "Certainly." A big, husky fellow was on the operating-table, unconscious, under ether. One of the best surgeons in France was performing the operation of trepanning. I could see the patient's brain, bare and beating, while the surgeon did his skilful work. Other doctors stood around, and three nurses, one an American girl, Miss Cowen, of Pittsburgh. "Will the man get well?" I asked the surgeon. "I hope so," he answered. "At all events, we shall do our best for him. You know, he is a German--c'est un Boche!"

On August 20, 1917, that very hospital, marked with the Red Cross, was bombed by German aeroplanes. One wing was set on fire. While the nurses and helpers were trying to rescue the patients, the bloody Potsdam vultures flew back and forth three times over the place, raking it with machine guns. More than thirty persons were killed, including doctors, German wounded, and one woman nurse.

God grant it was not the American girl! Yet why would not the killing of a French sister under the Red Cross be just as wicked?

Here I break off--uncompleted--my narration of the evil choice of war and the crimes in the conduct of war which have made the name of Germany abhorred.

The Allies, from the beginning, have pleaded for peace and fought for peace. America, obeying her conscience, has joined them in the conflict.

But what do we mean now by peace? We mean more than a mere cessation of hostilities. We mean that the burglar shall give back all that he has grabbed. We mean that the marauder shall make good all the damage that he has done. We mean that there shall be an open league of free democratic states, great and small, to guard against the recurrence of such a bloody calamity as the autocratic, militaristic Potsdam gang precipitated upon the world in 1914.

In the next chapter I shall discuss briefly the practical significance of this kind of peace and the absolute preconditions which must be realized before any conference on the subject will be profitable or even safe.

The duty of the present is to fight on beside France, Great Britain, Italy, Belgium, Servia, Roumania, and, we hope, Russia, "to bring the Government of the German Empire to terms and end the war."

To talk of any other course is treason, not only to our country but to the cause of true Peace.

Chapter VII
PAX HUMANA

I

The trouble with the ordinary or garden variety of pacifist is that he has a merely negative idea of peace.

The true idea of peace is positive, constructive, forward-looking. It is not content with a mere cessation of hostilities at any particular period of the world's history. It aims at the establishment of reason and justice as the rule of the world's life. It proposes to find the basis of this establishment in the freely expressed will of the peoples of the world.

The men and women who do the world's work are the sovereigns who must guarantee this real peace of the world.

That is what we are fighting for. Not pax Romana, nor pax Germanica, nor pax Britannica, but pax Humana--a peace which will bring a positive benefit to all the tribes of humanity.

Since the choice by the Imperial German Government, in August, 1914, of war as the means of settling international disputes, the Allies have been fighting against that choice and its bloody consequences. Every one of them--Great Britain, France, Italy, Russia--had pleaded for arbitration, conference, consultation, to avert this fearful conflict of arms. But it was in vain.

The United States of America, forced by the flagrant violation of its neutral rights to take an active part in the war, and led by its vital sympathies to the side of the Allies, committed by honor and conscience to the duty of fighting for a real peace of mankind, must carry on this war until its humane and democratic object is attained. To do less than that would be to renounce our place as a great nation, to deny our faith as Americans, and to expose our country to incalculable peril and disaster.

But now that all the nations of the earth have begun to realize the horror of this abominable German war, and to desire its ending, it is necessary for us, in conjunction with our friends of peaceful and democratic purpose, to consider, first, the conditions under which peace may be discussed with the Imperial German Government, and, second, the terms on which a peace may possibly be concluded.

II
THE CONDITIONS OF A PEACE CONFERENCE

We should distinguish clearly between the conditions which must be fulfilled before we can honorably enter into any talk of peace with our adversary, the begetter and beginner of this war; and the terms which the Allies and the United States and the other nations at war with Germany would put forward in such a conversation as a just and durable basis for the establishment of peace.

This distinction is essential. The conditions are antecedent and indispensable. Until they are fulfilled we cannot talk with the enemy, except in the language which he has chosen and forced upon us--the stern tongue of battle by land and sea.

Germany grandiloquently claims to be the first to propose a peace-conference as a substitute for the horrors of war. (See the Kaiser's note of December 12, 1916.[9])

She forgets the many proposals for such a conference which were made to her in the fateful month of July, 1914, by Servia, France, Great Britain, Italy, and Russia--all of which she contemptuously brushed aside in her scornful will to war. She forgets the offenses against international law and against the plain precepts of

---

9   This note contains not the slightest reference to the nature of the suggested peace. Its tone conforms to the orders which the Kaiser issued to his army on the same day: "Under the influence of the victory which you have gained by your bravery, I and the monarchs of the three states in alliance with me have made an offer of peace to the enemy. It is uncertain whether the object at which this offer is aimed will be reached. You will have meanwhile, with God's help, to continue to resist and defeat the enemy." It was not a proposal of peace. It was a proclamation of victory--German victory--and an invitation to surrender.

humanity which she has committed since that time and which have earned for her the indignation and mistrust of mankind. She forgets that her so-called proposal for a peace conference contained no suggestion of the terms of peace which she was willing to discuss. She forgets that such a proposal is a mere hypocritical mockery. No sane person, no intelligent nation, would enter into a conference without knowledge of the things to be considered.

This last point lies at the base of President Wilson's note of December 18, 1916, suggesting that the belligerent powers, on both sides, should "avow their respective views as to the terms upon which the war might be concluded and the arrangements which would be deemed satisfactory as a guarantee against its renewal or the kindling of any similar conflict in the future." This note, I believe, was sent to all the American Ambassadors and Ministers in Europe, with instructions to communicate it to the Governments to which they were accredited, whether belligerent or neutral.

Here is a point at which I can throw a little new light upon the situation. I handed the note, as I was ordered to do, to the Dutch Minister, without comment or recommendation. Almost immediately the German-subsidized press in Holland began to assail the Dutch Government for refusing to support President Wilson's note. It seemed to me that this was a falsehood, unjust to Holland, injurious to our Government, which had not asked for support. Therefore I made the following statement to the press on January 9, 1917:

"The Dutch Minister of Foreign Affairs is absolutely correct in saying that I handed him President Wilson's note of December 18 without any request or suggestion that the Netherlands Government should support it. I did so because I was so instructed by my Government. I was told to transmit the President's note simply as a matter of information. No request was added. The reason for this is because America understands the delicate and difficult position of the Netherlands Government, in the midst of the present war, and will not urge nor even ask it to do anything which it does not judge to be wise and prudent and helpful. I have done my best to promote this right understanding of the position of Holland in the United States, and I shall continue to do so. I have no knowledge of any instructions from Washington in regard to the manner of delivering the President's note in Spain.

"What I cannot understand is the general misunderstanding of that note. It expressly declared that it was not an offer of mediation nor a proposal of peace. It was simply a suggestion that the belligerents on both sides should state the terms on which they would be willing to consider and discuss peace. The Entente Powers have already done this with some clearness, and will probably soon do so even more clearly. The Central Powers have politely, even affectionately, but very practically, declined the President's invitation to state their terms. There is the deadlock on peace talk at present. When both sides are equally frank the world can judge whether the peace which all just men desire is near or far away."

The accuracy and propriety of this statement have never been questioned by the Department of State. On the contrary, it was practically affirmed by the President in his address to the Senate on January 22, 1917, when he said:

"On the 18th of December last I addressed an identic note to the Governments of the nations now at war, requesting them to state, more definitely than they had yet been stated by either group of belligerents, the terms upon which they would deem it possible to make peace. I spoke on behalf of humanity and of the rights of all neutral nations like our own, many of whose most vital interests the war puts in constant jeopardy.

"The Central Powers united in a reply which stated merely that they were ready to meet their antagonists in conference to discuss terms of peace.

"The Entente Powers have replied much more definitely and have stated, in general terms indeed, but with sufficient definiteness to imply details, the arrangements, guarantees, and acts of reparation which they deem to be indispensable conditions of a satisfactory settlement." Here, then, we come within sight of the first of the conditions which are absolutely precedent, at least so far as America is concerned, to any discussion of peace.

1. Germany must answer President Wilson's note of December 18, 1916. She must state her terms of peace, maximum or minimum, frankly and unequivocally.

Germany asserts that she is waging a defensive war. She must tell the world what she is defending. That she has never been willing to do.

Germany asserts that she is victorious thus far. She must say what she thinks her "victories" mean, and what they entitle her to claim and keep.

In brief, Germany must lay her cards on the table. If she wants peace--and certainly she needs it,--she must be willing to say what she means by it.

2. The second condition precedent to any discussion of peace terms with Germany has been clearly defined by President Wilson in his reply to the note issued by His Holiness Pope Benedict.

That reply was thoroughly sympathetic and conciliatory. Among its frank and strong paragraphs there was one which must be particularly noted:

"We cannot take the word of the present rulers of Germany as a guarantee of anything that is to endure unless explicitly supported by such conclusive evidence of the will and purpose of the German people themselves as the other peoples of the world would be justified in accepting. Without such guarantees treaties of settlement, agreements for disarmament, covenants to set up arbitration in the place of force, territorial adjustments, reconstitutions of small nations, if made with the German Government, no man, no nation, could now depend on."

Understand--this is not a flat refusal to treat with the House of Hohenzollern in any circumstances, which the more rabid and less thoughtful newspapers of England have urged. It is merely a statement that the rulers of Germany must have behind them a sufficient and explicit mandate and guarantee of the people of Germany before we can trust them.

We do not presume to interfere in the internal affairs of the German Empire. The people of that empire have a right to say how they shall be ruled. If they like the Hohenzollerns, good!

All that we ask is some clear, democratic guarantee of the German people behind the word of its chosen Government.

Does this mean a complete reformation of the German Empire, which in effect now consists of twenty-two hereditary kings, princes, dukes, and grand dukes, with the Kaiser at the head? Does it mean a constitutional remoulding of the empire?

That would be a long process. The people of Germany are well disciplined. There is small prospect of a revolution in that country unless war compels it.

What is it that we are pledged by President Wilson's statement to insist upon as a precondition of any peace conference with Germany? Simply this--that behind the word of the Kaiser there must be the word of the German people.

That word must be given in advance and in a way which will satisfy both the Allies and the United States. It is for the German people to find the way.

We cannot honorably talk peace with Germany until that way is found.

3. The third condition antecedent to a conference on peace is the renunciation and abandonment of the German submarine warfare upon merchant shipping.

On this point I do not speak with any kind of authority or official sanction. What I say is based, indeed, upon words uttered with the highest authority. But the conclusion drawn from them is merely my own judgment and has no force beyond that of the reasoning that has led me to it.

The American position in regard to this submarine warfare--its illegality, its inhumanity--has been clearly and eloquently defined by our Government again and again.

"The Government of the United States has been apprised that the Imperial German Government considered themselves to be obliged, by the extraordinary circumstances of the present war and the measures adopted by their adversaries in seeking to cut Germany off from all commerce, to adopt methods of retaliation which go much beyond the ordinary methods of warfare at sea, in the proclamation of a war zone from which they have warned neutral ships to keep away. This Government has already taken occasion to inform the Imperial German Government that it cannot admit the adoption of such measures or such a warning of danger to operate as in any degree an abbreviation of the rights of American shipmasters or of American citizens bound on lawful errands as passengers on merchant ships of belligerent neutrality; and that it must hold the Imperial German Government to a strict accountability for any infringement of those rights, intentional or incidental. It does not understand the Imperial German Government to question those rights. It assumes, on the contrary, that the Imperial German Government accept, as of course, the rule that the lives of non-combatants, whether they be of neutral citizenship or citizens of one of the nations at war, cannot lawfully or rightfully be put in jeopardy by the capture or destruction of an unarmed merchantman, and recognize also, as all other nations do, the obligation to take the usual precaution of visit and search to ascertain whether a suspected merchantman is in fact of belligerent nationality or is in fact carrying contraband of war under a neutral flag." (The Secretary of State, Washington, D. C., to the German Minister for Foreign Affairs, May 13, 1915.)

"The fact that more than one hundred American citizens were among those who perished" (reference to the sinking of the Lusitania) "made it the duty of the

Government of the United States to speak of these things and once more, with solemn emphasis, to call the attention of the Imperial German Government to the grave responsibility which the Government of the United States conceives that it has incurred in this tragic occurrence, and to the indisputable principle upon which that responsibility rests. The Government of the United States is contending for something much greater than mere rights of property or privileges of commerce. It is contending for nothing less high and sacred than the rights of humanity, which every government honors itself in respecting and which no government is justified in resigning on behalf of those under its care and authority." (The Secretary of State, Washington, D. C., to the German Minister for Foreign Affairs, June 9, 1915.)

"If a belligerent cannot retaliate against an enemy without injuring the lives of neutrals as well as their property, humanity, as well as justice and a due regard for the dignity of neutral powers, should dictate that the practice be discontinued. If persisted in it would in such circumstances constitute an unpardonable offense against the sovereignty of the neutral nation affected. . . . The rights of neutrals in time of war are based upon principle, not upon expediency, and the principles are immutable. It is the duty and obligation of belligerents to find a way to adapt the new circumstances to them." (The Secretary of State, Washington, D. C., to the German Minister for Foreign Affairs, July 21, 1915.)

"The law of nations in these matters, upon which the Government of the United States based that protest" (i.e., against the German declaration of February, 1915, declaring the danger zone around Great Britain and Ireland) "is not of recent origin or founded upon merely arbitrary principles set up by convention. It is based, on the contrary, upon manifest principles of humanity and has long been established with the approval and by the express assent of all civilized nations. . . . It has become painfully evident to it (the Government of the United States) that the position which it took at the very outset is inevitable, namely--the use of submarines for the destruction of an enemy's commerce is, of necessity, because of the very character of the vessels employed and the very methods of attack which their employment of course involves, utterly incompatible with the principles of humanity, the long-established and incontrovertible rights of neutrals, and the sacred immunities of non-combatants." (The Secretary of State, Washington, D. C., to the German Minister for Foreign Affairs, April 18, 1916.)

"But we cannot forget that we are in some sort and by the force of circumstances the responsible spokesmen of the rights of humanity, and that we cannot remain silent while those rights seem in process of being swept away in the maelstrom of this terrible war. We owe it to a due regard for our own rights as a nation, to our sense of duty as a representative of the rights of neutrals the world over, and to a just conception of the rights of mankind to take this stand now with the utmost solemnity and firmness." (President Wilson's Address to Congress, April 19, 1916.)

"The present German warfare against commerce is a warfare against mankind. It is a war against all nations. American ships have been sunk, American lives taken, in ways which it has stirred us very deeply to learn of, but the ships and people of other neutral and friendly nations have been sunk and overwhelmed in the waters in the same way. There has been no discrimination. The challenge is to all mankind. Each nation must decide for itself how it will meet it." (President Wilson's Message to Congress, April 2, 1917.)

The United States cannot go back on these words. They are fundamental in our position. I do not know whether the Allies have formally indorsed them or not. But that makes no difference. It seems to me that for America, with her traditional, unalterable devotion to the doctrine of Mare Liberum, as Grotius stated it, there can be no peace conference with a Government which is in active and flagrant violation of that principle.

I think that for us at least--we do not venture to speak for the Allies, though we believe they sympathize with our point of view--there can be no peace parley with Germany until she renounces and abandons her atrocious method of submarine warfare on merchant shipping.

Here, then, are the three conditions which ought to be fulfilled before we can honorably enter a conference on peace with the Imperial German Government. The first is a legitimate inference from the statements of the President. The second has been positively laid down by the President. The third is drawn, purely on my own responsibility, from his words.

First, Germany should frankly declare the aims with which she began this war, and the purposes with which she continues it on the territories which she has invaded.

Second, Germany must offer adequate guarantees that in any peace negotiations her rulers shall speak only and absolutely with the voice of the people behind them--in other words, with a democratic, not an autocratic, sanction.

Third, Germany ought to give a pledge of good faith by the abandonment of her illegal and inhuman submarine warfare on the merchant shipping of the world.

Is it likely that the predatory Potsdam gang will be willing to accept these three conditions soon?

I frankly confess that I do not know. Germany is in sore straits. That I know from personal observation. But I know also that she is magnificently organized, trained, and disciplined for obedience to the imperial will. She will carry her fight for world empire to the last limit.

When that limit is reached, when the German people know that the attempt of their rulers to dominate the world by war has failed, then it will be time to talk with them about the terms of peace.

III
THE TERMS OF PEACE

This is a long subject; and for that reason I mean to make it a short chapter.

1. A discussion of peace terms with our enemy, the Imperial German Government, is neither desirable nor safe under the present conditions.

Until that Government is disabused of the delusion that it has won, is winning, or will win a substantial victory in this war, it is not likely to say anything sane or reasonable about peace. A pax Germanica is what it is willing to discuss.

But that is just what we do not want. To enter such a discussion now would be both futile and perilous.

It would probably postpone the coming of that real pax humana for which the Allies have already made such great sacrifices, and for which we have pledged ourselves to fight at their side.

But meantime it is wise and right and useful to let the German people know, by such means as we can find, that we have not entered this war in the spirit of revenge or conquest, and that their annihilation or enslavement is not among the ends which we contemplate.

An admirable opportunity to give this humane and prudent assurance was of-fered by the Pope's proposal of a Peace Conference (August, 1917). President Wil-son, with characteristic acuteness and candor, made good use of this opportunity. While declining the proposal clearly and firmly, as impossible under the present conditions, he added the following statement of the peace purposes of the United States--a statement which approaches a definition by the process of exclusion:

"Punitive damages, the dismemberment of empires, the establishment of self-ish and exclusive economic leagues, we deem inexpedient, and in the end worse than futile, no proper basis for a peace of any kind, least of all for an enduring peace, that must be based upon justice and fairness and the common rights of mankind." (President Wilson's Note to His Holiness the Pope, August 27, 1917.)

Thus far (and in my judgment no farther) we may go in an indirect, third-personal discussion of the terms of peace with our enemy.

2. On the other hand, a full discussion of the terms of peace with our friends, the allied nations, will be most profitable--indeed, it is absolutely necessary.

The sooner it comes--the more frank, thorough, and confidential it is--the bet-ter!

The Allies, as President Wilson said in the address already quoted (January 22, 1917), have stated their terms of peace "with sufficient definiteness to imply details."

These terms have been summed up again and again in three general words:

RESTITUTION,
REPARATION,
GUARANTEES FOR THE FUTURE.

It is for us to discuss the details which are implied in these terms, not with our enemy, but with our friends who have borne the brunt of this German war against peace.

Nothing which would make their sacrifice vain could ever satisfy the heart and conscience of the United States.

We cannot honorably accept a peace which would leave Belgium, Luxembourg,

Servia, Montenegro, Roumania crushed and helpless in the hands of their captors.

We cannot honorably accept a peace which would leave our sister-republic France hopelessly exposed to the same kind of an assault which Germany made upon her in 1870 and in 1914.

We cannot honorably accept a peace which would leave Great Britain crippled and powerless to work with us in the maintenance of the freedom of the sea.

We cannot honorably accept a peace which would leave the Italian demand for unity unsatisfied, and the new Russian Republic helpless before its foes. Such, it seems to me, are the principles which must guide and govern us in the coming conference with our friends about the terms of peace.

In regard to the right of the peoples of the world, small or great, to determine their own form of government and their own action, we are fully committed. This principle is fundamental to our existence as a nation. President Wilson has reaffirmed it again and again, never more clearly or significantly than in his address to the Senate on January 22, 1917.

"And there is a deeper thing involved than even equality of rights among organized nations. No peace can last which does not recognize and accept the principle that governments derive all their just powers from the consent of the governed, and that no right anywhere exists to hand people about from sovereignty to sovereignty as if they were property.

"I take it for granted, for instance, if I may venture upon a single example, that statesmen everywhere are agreed that there should be a united, independent, and autonomous Poland, and that henceforth inviolable security of life, of worship, and of industrial and social development should be guaranteed to all peoples who have lived hitherto under the power of governments devoted to a faith and purpose hostile to their own."

This "example" must be interpreted in its full bearing upon all the questions which are likely to come up in the conference in regard to the terms of peace.

There is one more fixed point in the terms of a peace which the United States and the Allies can accept with honor. That is the formation, after this war is ended, of a compact, an alliance, a league, a union--call it what you will--of free democratic nations, pledged to use their combined forces, diplomatic, economic, and military, against the beginning of war by any nation which has not previously submitted its cause to international inquiry, conciliation, arbitration, or judicial hearing.

Here, again, experience enables me to throw a little new light upon the situation. In November, 1914, on my way home to America for surgical treatment, I had the privilege of conveying a personal, unofficial message to Washington from the British Minister of Foreign Affairs, Sir Edward (now Viscount) Grey. Remember, at this time America was neutral, and the "League to Enforce Peace" had not been formed.

This was the substance of the message: "The presence and influence of America in the council of peace after the war will be most welcome to us provided we can be assured of two things: First, that America stands for the restoration of all that Germany has seized in Belgium and France. Second, that America will enter and support, by force if necessary, a league of nations pledged to resist and punish any war begun without previous submission of the cause to international investigation and judgment."

This was the message that I took to Washington in 1914. Since that time the "League to Enforce Peace" has been organized in America (June 17, 1915). In my opinion it would be better named the "League to Defend Peace." But the name makes little difference. It is the principle, the idea, that counts.

This idea has been publicly approved by the leading spokesmen of all the allied nations, and notably by President Wilson in his speech at the League banquet, May 27, 1916, and in his address to the Senate, January 22, 1917, in which he said:

"Mere terms of peace between the belligerents will not satisfy even the belligerents themselves. Mere agreements may not make peace secure. It will be absolutely necessary that a force be created as a guarantor of the permanency of the settlement so much greater than the force of any nation now engaged in any alliance hitherto formed or projected that no nation, no probable combination of nations, could face or withstand it. If the peace presently to be made is to endure it must be a peace made secure by the organized major force of mankind."

Consider for a moment what such an organization would mean.

It would mean, first of all, the strongest possible condemnation of the attitude and action of Germany and her assistants in plotting, choosing, beginning, and forcing the present war upon the world.

It is precisely because she disdained and refused to submit the Austro-Servian quarrel, and her own secret plans and purposes to investigation, conference, judicial inquiry, that her blood-guiltiness is most flagrant, and her criminal assault upon the world's peace cries to Heaven for punishment.

Moreover, such an organization of free democratic states would mean a practical step toward a new era of international relations. It would amount, in effect, to what Premier Ribot, in his recent address at the anniversary of the battle of the Marne, called "a league of common defense." It would be a new kind of treaty of alliance--open, not secret--made by peoples, not by monarchs--an alliance against wars of aggression and conquest--an alliance against all wars whose beginners are unwilling to submit their cause to the common judgment of mankind. Such an open treaty of defense would practically condemn and cancel all secret treaties for offensive war as treasonable conspiracies against the commonwealth of the world.

But would the organization of such a league of nations to defend peace make war henceforward impossible?

No sane man, who knows the ignorance, the imperfection, the passionate frailty of human nature entertains such a wild dream or makes such an extravagant claim.

All that the league can hope to do is to make an aggressive war, such as Germany thrust upon the world in 1914, more difficult and more dangerous. All that it purposes is to set up a new safeguard of peace, based upon justice, and supported by the common faith, the collective force, and the mutual trust of democratic peoples.

That is one of the things--yes, I think it is the most important thing--for which we are now fighting with the Allies against Germany and her assistants:

PEACE WITH POWER.

These pages have been written as a voluntary contribution to the cause of our country in this righteous war against war. I should have been happier if my active service at the front could have been accepted. But since my age made that impossible I have tried, and shall go on trying, to do what I can in other ways to help our fight for real peace.

I close this bit of work with the noble lines of Tennyson:

"I would that wars should cease,
I would the globe from end to end
  Might sow and reap in peace,
And some new Spirit o'erbear the old,
  Or Trade refrain the Powers
From war with kindly links of gold,
  Or Love with wreaths of flowers.
Slav, Teuton, Kelt, I count them all
  My friends and brother souls,
With all the peoples, great and small,
  That wheel between the poles.
But since our mortal shadow, Ill,
  To waste this earth began--
Perchance from some abuse of Will
  In worlds before the man
Involving ours--he needs must fight
  To make true peace his own,
He needs must combat might with might,
  Or Might would rule alone."

www.bookjungle.com *email: sales@bookjungle.com fax: 630-214-0564 mail: Book Jungle PO Box 2226 Champaign, IL 61825*

The Codes Of Hammurabi And Moses
W. W. Davies

QTY

The discovery of the Hammurabi Code is one of the greatest achievements of archaeology, and is of paramount interest, not only to the student of the Bible, but also to all those interested in ancient history...

Religion   **ISBN:** *1-59462-338-4*   **Pages:**132

MSRP $12.95

The Theory of Moral Sentiments
Adam Smith

QTY

This work from 1749. contains original theories of conscience amd moral judgment and it is the foundation for systemof morals.

Philosophy **ISBN:** *1-59462-777-0*   **Pages:**536

MSRP $19.95

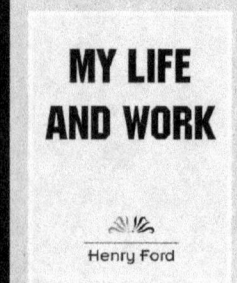

Jessica's First Prayer
Hesba Stretton

QTY

In a screened and secluded corner of one of the many railway-bridges which span the streets of London there could be seen a few years ago, from five o'clock every morning until half past eight, a tidily set-out coffee-stall, consisting of a trestle and board, upon which stood two large tin cans, with a small fire of charcoal burning under each so as to keep the coffee boiling during the early hours of the morning when the work-people were thronging into the city on their way to their daily toil...

Childrens   **ISBN:** *1-59462-373-2*   **Pages:**84

MSRP $9.95

My Life and Work
Henry Ford

QTY

Henry Ford revolutionized the world with his implementation of mass production for the Model T automobile. Gain valuable business insight into his life and work with his own auto-biography... "We have only started on our development of our country we have not as yet, with all our talk of wonderful progress, done more than scratch the surface. The progress has been wonderful enough but..."

Biographies/   **ISBN:** *1-59462-198-5*   **Pages:**300

MSRP $21.95

The Art of Cross-Examination
Francis Wellman

QTY

I presume it is the experience of every author, after his first book is published upon an important subject, to be almost overwhelmed with a wealth of ideas and illustrations which could readily have been included in his book, and which to his own mind, at least, seem to make a second edition inevitable. Such certainly was the case with me; and when the first edition had reached its sixth impression in five months, I rejoiced to learn that it seemed to my publishers that the book had met with a sufficiently favorable reception to justify a second and considerably enlarged edition. ..

Reference   **ISBN:** *1-59462-647-2*

Pages:412

MSRP $19.95

On the Duty of Civil Disobedience
Henry David Thoreau

QTY

Thoreau wrote his famous essay, On the Duty of Civil Disobedience, as a protest against an unjust but popular war and the immoral but popular institution of slave-owning. He did more than write—he declined to pay his taxes, and was hauled off to gaol in consequence. Who can say how much this refusal of his hastened the end of the war and of slavery ?

Law   **ISBN:** *1-59462-747-9*

Pages:48

MSRP $7.45

Dream Psychology Psychoanalysis for Beginners
Sigmund Freud

QTY

Sigmund Freud, born Sigismund Schlomo Freud (May 6, 1856 - September 23, 1939), was a Jewish-Austrian neurologist and psychiatrist who co-founded the psychoanalytic school of psychology. Freud is best known for his theories of the unconscious mind, especially involving the mechanism of repression; his redefinition of sexual desire as mobile and directed towards a wide variety of objects; and his therapeutic techniques, especially his understanding of transference in the therapeutic relationship and the presumed value of dreams as sources of insight into unconscious desires.

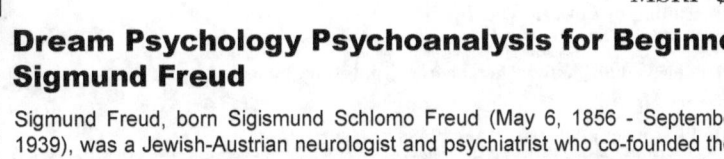

Psychology   **ISBN:** *1-59462-905-6*

Pages:196

MSRP $15.45

The Miracle of Right Thought
Orison Swett Marden

QTY

Believe with all of your heart that you will do what you were made to do. When the mind has once formed the habit of holding cheerful, happy, prosperous pictures, it will not be easy to form the opposite habit. It does not matter how improbable or how far away this realization may see, or how dark the prospects may be, if we visualize them as best we can, as vividly as possible, hold tenaciously to them and vigorously struggle to attain them, they will gradually become actualized, realized in the life. But a desire, a longing without endeavor, a yearning abandoned or held indifferently will vanish without realization.

Pages:360

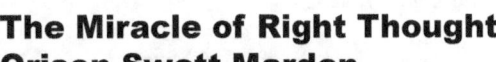

Self Help   **ISBN:** *1-59462-644-8*

MSRP $25.45

The Rosicrucian Cosmo-Conception Mystic Christianity *by Max Heindel*   ISBN: *1-59462-188-8* **$38.95**
The Rosicrucian Cosmo-conception is not dogmatic, neither does it appeal to any other authority than the reason of the student. It is: not controversial, but is: sent forth in the, hope that it may help to clear..
New Age/Religion Pages 646

Abandonment To Divine Providence *by Jean-Pierre de Caussade*   ISBN: *1-59462-228-0* **$25.95**
"The Rev. Jean Pierre de Caussade was one of the most remarkable spiritual writers of the Society of Jesus in France in the 18th Century. His death took place at Toulouse in 1751. His works have gone through many editions and have been republished...
Inspirational/Religion Pages 400

Mental Chemistry *by Charles Haanel*   ISBN: *1-59462-192-6* **$23.95**
Mental Chemistry allows the change of material conditions by combining and appropriately utilizing the power of the mind. Much like applied chemistry creates something new and unique out of careful combinations of chemicals the mastery of mental chemistry...
New Age Pages 354

The Letters of Robert Browning and Elizabeth Barret Barrett 1845-1846 vol II   ISBN: *1-59462-193-4* **$35.95**
by Robert Browning and Elizabeth Barrett
Biographies Pages 596

Gleanings In Genesis (volume I) *by Arthur W. Pink*   ISBN: *1-59462-130-6* **$27.45**
Appropriately has Genesis been termed "the seed plot of the Bible" for in it we have, in germ form, almost all of the great doctrines which are afterwards fully developed in the books of Scripture which follow...
Religion/Inspirational Pages 420

The Master Key *by L. W. de Laurence*   ISBN: *1-59462-001-6* **$30.95**
In no branch of human knowledge has there been a more lively increase of the spirit of research during the past few years than in the study of Psychology, Concentration and Mental Discipline. The requests for authentic lessons in Thought Control, Mental Discipline and...   New Age/Business Pages 422

The Lesser Key Of Solomon Goetia *by L. W. de Laurence*   ISBN: *1-59462-092-X* **$9.95**
This translation of the first book of the "Lernegton" which is now for the first time made accessible to students of Talismanic Magic was done, after careful collation and edition, from numerous Ancient Manuscripts in Hebrew, Latin, and French...
New Age/Occult Pages 92

Rubaiyat Of Omar Khayyam *by Edward Fitzgerald*   ISBN: *1-59462-332-5* **$13.95**
Edward Fitzgerald, whom the world has already learned, in spite of his own efforts to remain within the shadow of anonymity, to look upon as one of the rarest poets of the century, was born at Bredfield, in Suffolk, on the 31st of March, 1809. He was the third son of John Purcell...   Music Pages 172

Ancient Law *by Henry Maine*   ISBN: *1-59462-128-4* **$29.95**
The chief object of the following pages is to indicate some of the earliest ideas of mankind, as they are reflected in Ancient Law, and to point out the relation of those ideas to modern thought.
Religiom/History Pages 452

Far-Away Stories *by William J. Locke*   ISBN: *1-59462-129-2* **$19.45**
"Good wine needs no bush, but a collection of mixed vintages does. And this book is just such a collection. Some of the stories I do not want to remain buried for ever in the museum files of dead magazine-numbers an author's not unpardonable vanity..."
Fiction Pages 272

Life of David Crockett *by David Crockett*   ISBN: *1-59462-250-7* **$27.45**
"Colonel David Crockett was one of the most remarkable men of the times in which he lived. Born in humble life, but gifted with a strong will, an indomitable courage, and unremitting perseverance...
Biographies/New Age Pages 424

Lip-Reading *by Edward Nitchie*   ISBN: *1-59462-206-X* **$25.95**
Edward B. Nitchie, founder of the New York School for the Hard of Hearing, now the Nitchie School of Lip-Reading, Inc, wrote "LIP-READING Principles and Practice". The development and perfecting of this meritorious work on lip-reading was an undertaking...   How-to Pages 400

A Handbook of Suggestive Therapeutics, Applied Hypnotism, Psychic Science   ISBN: *1-59462-214-0* **$24.95**
by Henry Munro
Health/New Age/Health/Self-help Pages 376

A Doll's House: and Two Other Plays *by Henrik Ibsen*   ISBN: *1-59462-112-8* **$19.95**
Henrik Ibsen created this classic when in revolutionary 1848 Rome. Introducing some striking concepts in playwriting for the realist genre, this play has been studied the world over.
Fiction/Classics/Plays 308

The Light of Asia *by sir Edwin Arnold*   ISBN: *1-59462-204-3* **$13.95**
In this poetic masterpiece, Edwin Arnold describes the life and teachings of Buddha. The man who was to become known as Buddha to the world was born as Prince Gautama of India but he rejected the worldly riches and abandoned the reigns of power when... Religion/History/Biographies Pages 170

The Complete Works of Guy de Maupassant *by Guy de Maupassant*   ISBN: *1-59462-157-8* **$16.95**
"For days and days, nights and nights, I had dreamed of that first kiss which was to consecrate our engagement, and I knew not on what spot I should put my lips..."
Fiction/Classics Pages 240

The Art of Cross-Examination *by Francis L. Wellman*   ISBN: *1-59462-309-0* **$26.95**
Written by a renowned trial lawyer, Wellman imparts his experience and uses case studies to explain how to use psychology to extract desired information through questioning.
How-to/Science/Reference Pages 408

Answered or Unanswered? *by Louisa Vaughan*   ISBN: *1-59462-248-5* **$10.95**
Miracles of Faith in China
Religion Pages 112

The Edinburgh Lectures on Mental Science (1909) *by Thomas*   ISBN: *1-59462-008-3* **$11.95**
This book contains the substance of a course of lectures recently given by the writer in the Queen Street Hall, Edinburgh. Its purpose is to indicate the Natural Principles governing the relation between Mental Action and Material Conditions...
New Age/Psychology Pages 148

Ayesha *by H. Rider Haggard*   ISBN: *1-59462-301-5* **$24.95**
Verily and indeed it is the unexpected that happens! Probably if there was one person upon the earth from whom the Editor of this, and of a certain previous history, did not expect to hear again...
Classics Pages 380

Ayala's Angel *by Anthony Trollope*   ISBN: *1-59462-352-X* **$29.95**
The two girls were both pretty, but Lucy who was twenty-one who supposed to be simple and comparatively unattractive, whereas Ayala was credited, as her Bombwhat romantic name might show, with poetic charm and a taste for romance. Ayala when her father died was nineteen...   Fiction Pages 484

The American Commonwealth *by James Bryce*   ISBN: *1-59462-286-3* **$34.45**
An interpretation of American democratic political theory. It examines political mechanics and society from the perspective of Scotsman James Bryce
Politics Pages 572

Stories of the Pilgrims *by Margaret P. Pumphrey*   ISBN: *1-59462-116-0* **$17.95**
This book explores pilgrims religious oppression in England as well as their escape to Holland and eventual crossing to America on the Mayflower, and their early days in New England...
History Pages 268

QTY

The Fasting Cure *by Sinclair Upton*   ISBN: *1-59462-222-1*   **$13.95**
In the Cosmopolitan Magazine for May, 1910, and in the Contemporary Review (London) for April, 1910, I published an article dealing with my experiences in fasting. I have written a great many magazine articles, but never one which attracted so much attention...   New Age/Self Help/Health Pages 164

Hebrew Astrology *by Sepharial*   ISBN: *1-59462-308-2*   **$13.45**
In these days of advanced thinking it is a matter of common observation that we have left many of the old landmarks behind and that we are now pressing forward to greater heights and to a wider horizon than that which represented the mind-content of our progenitors...   Astrology Pages 144

Thought Vibration or The Law of Attraction in the Thought World   ISBN: *1-59462-127-6*   **$12.95**
by William Walker Atkinson   Psychology/Religion Pages 144

Optimism *by Helen Keller*   ISBN: *1-59462-108-X*   **$15.95**
Helen Keller was blind, deaf, and mute since 19 months old, yet famously learned how to overcome these handicaps, communicate with the world, and spread her lectures promoting optimism. An inspiring read for everyone...   Biographies/Inspirational Pages 84

Sara Crewe *by Frances Burnett*   ISBN: *1-59462-360-0*   **$9.45**
In the first place, Miss Minchin lived in London. Her home was a large, dull, tall one, in a large, dull square, where all the houses were alike, and all the sparrows were alike, and where all the door-knockers made the same heavy sound...   Childrens/Classic Pages 88

The Autobiography of Benjamin Franklin *by Benjamin Franklin*   ISBN: *1-59462-135-7*   **$24.95**
The Autobiography of Benjamin Franklin has probably been more extensively read than any other American historical work, and no other book of its kind has had such ups and downs of fortune. Franklin lived for many years in England, where he was agent...   Biographies/History Pages 332

Name	
Email	
Telephone	
Address	
City, State ZIP	

☐ **Credit Card**   ☐ **Check / Money Order**

Credit Card Number	
Expiration Date	
Signature	

Please Mail to: Book Jungle
           PO Box 2226
           Champaign, IL 61825
or Fax to: 630-214-0564

ORDERING INFORMATION

web*: www.bookjungle.com*
email*: sales@bookjungle.com*
fax*: 630-214-0564*
mail*: Book Jungle PO Box 2226 Champaign, IL 61825*
or PayPal *to sales@bookjungle.com*

Please contact us for bulk discounts

DIRECT-ORDER TERMS

**20% Discount if You Order
Two or More Books**
Free Domestic Shipping!
Accepted: Master Card, Visa,
Discover, American Express

www.ingramcontent.com/pod-product-compliance
Lightning Source LLC
Chambersburg PA
CBHW082014170626

46817CB00009B/3102